Brazos shook his head slowly. "Mister, you're seven kinds of a fool."

"Quite. I could pull this trigger—kill you right now, and nobody would blame me." Lambeth's voice held its crisp precision, but his face was nearly bloodless. "But—honor, you know—a chap doesn't have a real choice. It's—it's got to be a fair fight." He gestured at a rear hallway. "Now then."

"For God's sake, no, Lambeth."

"Damn you, *yes*." Lambeth thumbed back the hammer, and, watching his eyes, Brazos knew the man had the insides to carry it through here and now. He accepted the choice with a gray fatalism, knowing that all odds even, he could easily take Lambeth in a gunfight. Suddenly the empty irony of it washed through him.

John Lambeth was the man he thought he'd come here to kill—and now—utterly against his will—he would be forced to . . .

A MAN
CALLED BRAZOS

by T. V. OLSEN

FAWCETT GOLD MEDAL • NEW YORK

A MAN CALLED BRAZOS

CHAPTER ONE

BRAZOS CAME ACROSS the pass into the south hills of the Two Troughs country while the late afternoon held softly warm with spring. He halted soon to rest the big blue roan, which had the green heaves after weeks of grain-feeding, and uncapped his battered old canteen. He took a mouthful of rancid water and spat it out. The hillsides were tinkling with muddy sun-shot freshets. He said, "Hell," with a dour finality, and dismounted and stretched out on his belly and drank deeply. The water was snow-cold and made his jaws ache.

Brazos filled his canteen, stood, and ran his hard glance to the tilting valley floor. Farther on it gave way to hilly meadows of wind-rippled young grass, and foothills shaggy with timber rose to the far purpled thrust of snow-veined peaks. Set in its deep isolation in the Sierra Diablo peaks, the Two Troughs basin held a vast, rich-grassed range connected by a spur line to an outside railhead. It also held, as he'd heard, a threat of trouble which was no damned business of his; he had all he needed, and was ready to oblige anyone who wanted some of it.

He was a short, wiry and spare-flanked man with a compact hardness through his chest and shoulders. His faded-rose shirt was threadbare, his old jeans colorless with wear and chalky at the knees, and both were oft-patched and fresh only in their unmended tears. His black slouch hat was battered shapeless, and his fiery hair burred out beneath it with a shaggy truculence.

His face was profiled like an Indian's, its light-complected skin burned to a deep ruddy-brown, with a big angular nose and pale eyes deeply socketed between a straight-ridged brow and high cheekbones. A scrub of bristling red beard, its stiff hairs tipped by sunlight, made his face wider than it was, accenting his wide full mouth. In temper the mouth settled to a tight insolent line, and then strongly matched his whole face. It was a face that a man might find toughly likable, but never pleasant.

Brazos' saddle and working gear were well-kept, better than his person, and so was his old six-gun with its black rubber grips and oiled worn leather of holster and brass-shelled belt. He was a man of practical care and no vanity but pride, and that self-contained and indifferent to outside opinion. He was not narrow; he'd had a bare three R's worth of schooling, but there were always two or more dog-eared books in his warsack and some self-learning had rubbed into his speech. Not that he gave a damn, his words were spare and seldom.

Mounting, he said to the blue, "All right, lift 'em now," and went down the rocky downtaper of the pass end, and came onto the grass hills with their skirmish lines of spruce, fir and small pine. The day was calm in its lateness; a few long-tailed jays flitted overhead, and squirrels chattered in the pines; a chicken hawk spiraled against the blue-steel sky.

Out of that stillness sheep bleated in panic; it startled him, and so did a bunched rattle of hoofs. He swung offtrail and angled to his right up a flanking hogback ridge, and came onto its tip. He saw a large flock of the woollies coming in a dusty pour down a stony arroyo with a rider pressing them hard, cutting his rope at their rumps. Where the banks shallowed down the animals scattered left and right in their stupid fear, blundering into dense tangles of brush. The rider pulled up his prancing mount and the sun hit his dark laughing face.

He was no sheepman, Brazos thought: a cowpoker for sure, long and lean in the saddle. It was hard to tell any more from here, and then the rider wheeled and turned back, and was lost beyond a screen of young fir. With only idle curiosity, having often worked cows and finding the roughing up of a herder and his hated woollies of less than no concern, Brazos came down into the arroyo and swung after the rider. Off ahead he heard the impatient lift of a man's voice:

"All right, Stu, put your rope on him."

Now, as he left the arroyo for a boulder-studded slope, he saw a man running directly toward him, with a rider following at a stretching lope. The man afoot, a young Mexican, pulled up short seeing Brazos, and in that moment the horseman whirled out his rope and dropped the loop cleanly over his shoulders. The rider spurred offside and the Mexican ran a few bucking steps before he was yanked flat; then dragged away. His incoherent yell ended in sharp pain as he bounced against a rock. Brazos saw the bright instant blood streak his shirt, but the rider didn't break pace.

Brazos didn't think about it. He simply yanked his rifle from scabbard, levered and hip-braced it, and shot. The wild slug whined off a boulder to the rider's right, near enough to set his horse rearing. While he fought, hoarsely cursing, for control of the sunfishing animal, Brazos settled his rifle on the other horsemen.

The man he'd first seen, a Texan by his rig and hat-crease, had dropped his hand to his pistol. It was pure reflex; he turned one soft oath off his tongue and did nothing. He was as long and dark as a blacksnake, with a saturnine face and cold shrewd eyes. He smelled like danger, and Brazos judged him a cowpoker by circumstance, not choice.

The same might be said of his partner, but it was harder to tell. He was lean as a cat, deceptively so, because he was a large man with weight through shoulders and chest. His eyes were of the palest blue, made sultry and expressionless by half-shuttered lids; his flaxen hair, which lay like a tight curling cap against his big head, was sun-faded nearly white. His face, broad and bland and almost handsome, was clean-shaven but for a hairline mustache, his lower lip oddly grooved by a deep scar which lent an ironic twist to his mouth, a faint lisp to his speech: "You want trouble, stud, you've piled up some fair makings."

"Shut up," Brazos said mildly, and looked at the cold-eyed man. "I'd think about that, I was you."

The man uncurled his fingers and settled his hand carefully to his pommel. He swore again. "That's fair," Brazos said, and to the rider tight-reining his skittish horse now, "Take your rope off him, Slim, and come over here."

The third man was chunky, with bright small eyes slitted between rolls of fat, but his clumsy squatness was offset by a thick musculature which bulged his soiled range clothes. They were slick and stiff with filth, and his hair was like dirty straw. His face screwed up as if he were ready to cry, a trick expression; there was nothing but brute fury in the way he dismounted, roughly yanked his rope free, then tramped over leading his horse.

Brazos watched the Mexican crawl to his hands and knees, cuddling his bloody-sleeved arm against his chest. He got to his feet and tossed back his lank black hair. He was a small man, and his long lantern-jawed face gave him the look of an ugly brown gnome. His eyes were alight with black rage as he tramped upslope and bent to pick up an old Kentucky long-flintlock laying in the grass.

"No," Brazos said.

7

"I mean to kill these *chingados*, senor."

"No."

"They would have—" the youth began hotly, then taking a second hard look at Brazos, let the butt of his old smoothbore drop to the ground. "I think I don't want to argue with a gringo with such a face."

"Scour your own pot," Brazos grunted dryly. "Most times I count a man's affairs his own, but a Dutch ride over rocks takes some damned strong reasons."

"Reason enough," the big man lisped, "if you don't mind my saying."

"Talk away."

"Nugget land here—"

"It's open range," the Mexican broke in hotly, "any man's grass."

"Cattleman's grass."

"My few sheep don't do no hurt—!"

"Your turn next," said Brazos. "All right, Nugget."

"Starr, Charley Starr. I ride for Nugget. There's an understanding about his foothill country. Government made its survey thirty years back and nobody's sure of the patented lines. Montalvo—a big greaser outfit over west—hogs most of the Two Troughs, public domain too. Montalvo looks after all the pepperbellies, like this one. Fine and good, so long as they stay out of these east foothills."

"Only since Nugget says so," the Mexican put in. "Always the open land here has been for the use of the little people. It was so in my father's time, in his father's."

"Only because Montalvo says so. The coin spins both ways, Mex."

Chunky Stu rumbled, "Sure," as his horse shifted restlessly.

"Slim," Brazos said thinly, "you're kind of high for my taste. Keep downwind and don't move around like that."

Charley Starr smiled. "What's your slice of this?"

"Nothing. Hell of an interesting caucus and all, but it gets nowhere." He tilted the rifle sharply, motioning the three Nugget men off.

"If there's a next time, Red," said Starr, "I'll see you first."

"Maybe. I'll be around."

Charley Starr said, "Fine, fine," and flung his horse around on a savage rein, the others following. Brazos watched them vanish down a slow dip of hills, and only then returned his rifle to its boot.

"That was a mistake, senor."

8

"Kane. Never shoot at another man's dogs."

The young Mexican's scowl smoothed; his white teeth smiled. "Pepe Garcia. Ha, that's right. Dogs. Where do you go now?"

"Camp."

Garcia lifted his rifle to the crook of his good arm and pointed with his bloody hand. "Over there's my place. When I got the sheep together, and if you don't mind pepperbelly grub, you should stay the night."

Brazos Kane looked at this sturdy runt of a man straight as a board in his pride, liking his honest ugly gnome's face. "All right, Garcia."

Pepe whistled between two fingers, and a large brown and white dog trotted out of the nearby firs. "Ah Jose, you lazy cowardly *bastardo*. Go get the sheep." The dog wagged shamelessly, and raced down the arroyo. "How quick he is gone when trouble comes," Pepe grumbled without rancor. "Wolves or men, it is the same. He will live a long time, that dog."

After a few minutes of barking, bleating and thrashing of brush, the whole flock came in sight with Jose worrying them furiously. "Take them home, you brave dog," Pepe said, and Brazos swung his horse alongside the man and dog, idly hazing the flock along.

The lowering sun barely rimmed the west peaks by the time they crossed two shallow ridges and entered the narrow valley where Pepe's cabin lay. It was built of green logs, with the rambling fold of cottonwood logs set off behind it enclosing a long stretch of pasture. Smoke spiraled into the still evening from a mud chimney, and then the smell of coffee and frying hogside was a sharp reminder to Brazos that he was damned sick of his own cookery.

Pepe, after turning his sheep into the fold, waited politely while Brazos watered the blue at a small spring, grained him from the saddle grainbag, and hobbled him out on the grass. Then they entered the cabin, where he met Pepe's wife. She was hardly more than a girl, as pretty in her dark way as Pepe was ugly, and she made a great fuss over his hurt arm. "She's a scratch only," Pepe said, but let her wash up the long tear in his biceps and tie it up, while he related the how of it.

She too was insistent that Brazos stay the night, but he felt a small guilt as he sat at the crude puncheon table on a halflog bench and looked around the one room with its clay floor, meager necessities, a few comforts, and the handcarved

9

cradle where a brown baby napped. The Garcias had little enough to spare; and his discomfort deepened when Pepe said grandly, "You will take our bed in the loft." He waved aside objections; there were worse beds than straw on a clay floor.

The fried salt pork and hot tortillas with green sauce were very good; he had to force himself to refuse their urgings of more, and when this mildly offended them, couldn't turn down second and third cups of coffee. While Juana cleared the table, Pepe produced two cigarillos obviously hoarded against a great occasion, lighted Brazos' and then his own with a flourish, and said: "You are looking for work someplace, eh?"

"Maybe." Brazos was noncommittal, eying the glowing tip of his cigarillo. "There's a man, Pepe. Have reason to believe he's here in the Two Troughs country. You might know of him. An Anglo, pale, very tall and thin. Light hair and blue eyes. A man of manners, with a foreign accent."

"His name?"

"Wish I could say. No idea myself."

Pepe cocked a brow shrewdly. "Then he is no friend of yours, this man."

"Haven't met him," Brazos said evasively.

"Ah. There's such a man as you describe. Mister Lambeth. The prize three you saw today work for him."

"He owns this Nugget outfit?"

"Ah."

Brazos leaned forward, settling his crossed arms on the table. "I want to know about him, Pepe. When he came here and where from, his financial condition—"

"Que?"

"How much money he has. He make free with it? Spend big?"

"Ha, si." Pepe screwed up his face, squinting at the clay fireplace whose dancing light played softly through the semi-gloom. "I don' know where he come from, but it was maybe, uh, three month ago. Nugget was then only one of a whole bunch of hardscrabble Anglo outfits over in the east basin. This Mister Lambeth bought out some little outfits at their own prices, also the Nugget which old Jay Barstow had built to a middling size. Old Jay had died. His son wanted to sell out and go East. Now, together, all these outfits make one— maybe a half, maybe a third, as big as Montalvo." Pepe drew gently on his cigarillo, slowly nodding. "That is when the trouble start."

"Two big dogs tussling over one bone, eh?"

"Ah. It was different when there was only Montalvo and the little ranches. Montalvo, senor—there has always been Montalvo. They were the blood of grandees. The first Montalvo got grant of all this basin two hundred years ago from the king of Spain. After cession to the Americanos there was great fuss over if the old Spanish grants held water. The territory court of New Mexico let Don Diego Montalvo keep half his former land. This, the west basin of Two Troughs. Various Anglos stake their claims over east. But still Montalvo held the open range, the good summer grass under the Diablos. Montalvo was the power, much wealth, many riders. But always they use the power well, protecting all the Mexican people here. In the old days we all worked for Montalvo; times change, but the good customs don't. Senor O'Brien has kept them for us; all us little hombres share open range with Montalvo." Pepe chuckled, and coughed on some wrong-way smoke. "How the Anglos hate that."

"O'Brien? Sounds Anglo himself."

"Ah. Don Diego had no sons; Senor Mike O'Brien who worked his way to foreman of Montalvo, married the one daughter. When Don Diego dies it all goes to Senora Maria, and she died shortly after bearing her first child. Again there is only one daughter, who is half Anglo; it is supposed she will marry an Anglo one day, and then . . . Senor Mike has kept the old ways well but he is as one of us. When he too is gone, who knows?" Pepe slightly lifted his hands from the table and shrugged.

"And who's pushing the other," Brazos asked idly, "Montalvo or Nugget?"

Pepe's brow puckered. "It is not easy to say. How is it when there are abruptly two big dogs, as you call them, where there was one? And one juicy bone between them? Maybe they can't help themselves; up go the hackles. Maybe, I think, that's it. Senor Mike is a tough man, surely not a mean one, though he talks mean, to be sure. He'll fight to hold the open range he claims, but not push for more."

"Lambeth?" Brazos now caught himself leaning intently forward and he slacked deliberately back; it was this answer that interested him.

Pepe's laugh was a deprecating snort. "That one is not even tough; he is a gentleman. That too is a strength maybe, sometimes, but I do not call this Lambeth strong." Brazos waited through a hesitant pause, and again Pepe shrugged. "It is hard to say, since I have seen this Lambeth three, four

11

times only. I don' know that a man should call him weak. He is like you though, I think—a good Anglo."

Brazos scowled at a crack in the table. It was not what he wanted to hear; he needed to be sure of his man.

Pepe sighed deeply. "If it breaks, there will come one bloody bath in this basin—Anglos against Mexicans. The feeling has built a long while, and it needed only such a thing as a big outfit also on the Anglo side to bring it to a head."

Little Luis in his cradle woke and wailed; Juana quit the dishes and picked him up, soothing him in liquid Spanish. She sat at the table and bared a smooth brown shoulder and breast and let him nurse. They smiled at his greedy suckling, and Pepe said fondly, "Ah, the good boy; such fare makes strong men." He gave Brazos a raffish wink, then promptly turned the coin over to a formal courtesy. "My pardon, senor; the day has been long, and you're tired."

Brazos made an uneasy protest as Pepe lighted the single lamp and led the way up the ladder to the loft. His reply was full of somber pride. "The welcome of our house, she's always yours. You will be around a time, eh?"

"A time." They stood erect in the loft, facing each other in the lampglow, and he lowered his voice. "Better say this so you won't take it amiss later. Spring gather coming up, the local outfits'll be taking on riders."

"That is so."

"I aim to try Nugget."

He expected quick resentment, but Pepe only gave a slow shrewd nod. "It has to do with this man you look for?"

"Yes."

Pepe sighed. "A man does what he must. But I should hate it to put us on different sides when the trouble comes. For sure, it will come. Good night, senor."

CHAPTER TWO

AS THE FIRST FLUSH of dawn flooded the far peaks, Brazos rode the blue roan up to the cabin door, where Pepe gave him directions for reaching Nugget. Juana stood by holding the small Luis, who loudly cooed and gave Brazos' extended finger a husky tug. "He says come back soon," Pepe grinned broadly. "You will go with God, my friend."

Brazos looked back once, topping the first shallow ridge above the valley, and the Garcias were still there; they waved, and he briefly lifted a hand and went on. He felt oddly warmed and was irritated by it; he made none-too-congenial company, and their liking could be put down to gratitude. Still the warmth of pride and love he'd seen under that ramshackle roof touched him oddly. Pepe was a poor man, but he had something . . . Brazos let his thoughts harden to indrawn bleakness. *Well, we're downtrail, Pop; just a little longer.*

At that, though, he had to grin, for Pop Melaven had been, in his slack and footloose indifference, a man of timeless patience. He'd thought like an outcast Indian and had lived like one. He had looked enough like one to fool Brazos on the long-gone day when he, a dirty-faced foul-mouthed kid, had sneaked into the livery stable stall where Pop was sprawled in a heap of straw, apparently dead drunk. Pop had been drunk, all right; he was drunk whenever he had money, but as he'd said, "Takes a hell of a load to faze me out; man gets pickled and preserved."

Brazos, orphaned at ten by a Choctaw raiding party, had afterward been farmed out to a crusty uncle, a Kansas farmer who made too free with his razor strop on a boy's backside. Brazos had left through a back window one dark night and hadn't stopped till he reached a railhead town a hundred miles away. There he had lived for a year, mostly by his wits and petty stealing. There were few odd jobs, especially for an undersized ragheel kid; but in a wide-open trail town there were always alley-prone drunks to be rolled, or at the worst, scraps to be filched from garbage pails.

That night, as he was rifling through the sodden old

horse-trapper's gear, Pop Melaven's sinewy hand had shot suddenly out of the straw and grabbed him. After asking only Brazos' name, he'd rasped, "I'm a man hates fences and roofs, and towns is only good to get drunk in. Wouldn't turn a yaller dog over to the goddam law, but nothing to say I can't lick you bloody." Brazos had cursed him, and Pop's grin had showed his stained and broken teeth. " 'Less you want to side along with me and work. And boy, I'll work your ass to the bare bone of it. Flay 'er off or slave 'er off, it's one to me. Up to you." He'd rubbed his brass-studded belt, and Brazos was two seconds in making up his mind.

Pop had been as good as his word. In the days that followed, Brazos grew bitterly accustomed to sweating under a broiling sun, building fence across canyon mouths, using a shovel, swinging an ax, handling every detail of the camp chores while Pop loafed in the shade and consumed a couple gallons of whiskey. Then began what Pop called the real work, driving the wild horses to trap.

It had marked Brazos' first glimmer of respect for the mustanger; there was no nonsense about Pop Melaven when he buckled down. Sharp-eyed and sober then, he was a tireless tracker and a master of his tradeslore. His reprimands were harsh and his praise nonexistent, but he'd never treated his protégé as less than a partner in harness.

On the day when they'd driven the rough-broken string to town and found a buyer, Pop had thrust part of the money into Brazos' fist: "Get y'rself a bath and some new duds. You know what our camp needs is; buy 'em up, and any pretties you got a hanker after. Too bad you got just enough to pee with." Then he'd given a hitch to his pants, chuckled, and headed for the nearest brothel.

It had been the whole story of their partnership since. Over ten years it had become a way of life, so that he'd come to give only passing thought to Pop's whoring and drinking up half their hard-earned proceeds, or to handling the bulk of menial work, even after his trade experience matched Pop's. And, for a boy, there was the life of unbridled freedom that all boys coveted. He'd given little thought to the fact of their relation, though feeling ran deep with habit. Odd now to think that he'd never known Pop Melaven's first name or a hint of his past or even his approximate age. He'd had the young-old look that combined a plainsman's rigorous health with the ravages of hard drinking. It was easy to anticipate a brutal and bitter end for the man, and yet when it came it had dropped the bottom out of Brazos' life.

14

It had been by far the biggest horse gather they'd ever made, working the stony hills above Las Truchas down by the border for nearly a year with a crew of Mexican wranglers. By now the balance of authority had shifted, Pop Melaven slackly and amiably following Brazos' lead. And Brazos' whole ambition was to buy and develop a horse ranch and cross Morgan stock with the wild stuff. He couldn't make Pop less than a full partner, though he'd known that Pop's ready agreement to the plan meant Pop's eye to the notion that a steady business would enable him to stay steadily drunk. As they'd built up the big gather and as word got around, prospective buyers visited their camp, vying with offers. Brazos continued to hold out for the best price.

One day when he was out of camp, Pop Melaven had accepted the check of an oft-visiting buyer for the entire horse herd. Then Pop promptly rode into Las Truchas to cash it. Brazos judged that the long and liquorless months of grueling work had simply soured Pop into rebellion. He was found in an alley the next morning, with the back of his skull crushed.

Seeley, the day bartender at the Silver Belle saloon, could tell Brazos only that Pop had spent all the previous afternoon drinking with an itinerant gambler; the barroom had been deserted except for the three of them. Pop had waved fistfuls of money while giving loud bragging replies to the gambler's soft probing questions. No, Seeley hadn't caught the gambler's name; he'd drifted into town the day before and had had one near shootout with a ranchhand who'd accused him of bellystripping. At dusk Pop had left the Silver Belle to sleep it off somewhere and the gambler had left a minute or two afterward. Nobody had seen him since, nor the twelve thousand in greenbacks that had gone out stuffed carelessly in Pop Melaven's pockets.

The gambler's description, as Seeley gave it, was a distinctive one, but there was no way to follow it up. For the next several months he'd stuck like a burr to the Las Truchas area, wringing every shred of gossip for a chance clue. Finally he'd heard from a grubline drifter about an English-sounding fellow named John Lambeth who'd bought out a flock of outfits up in the Two Troughs country near Soledad. Lambeth's description matched in detail that which Seeley had given of the gambler, but other descriptions he'd winnowed out were also close: it was only now, when he jogged the bartender with the name of Two Troughs, that Seeley, who had a memory like a leaky bucket, recalled the gambler's

15

mention of that country the first day he'd arrived . . . "I remember, by God. I mentioned the Two Troughs basin somehow—we was talking—and he said he was moseying up that way from here. Business, he told me."

Three months ago, Pepe said. That would be about right. Assuming that Lambeth had already accumulated a sizable stake—which could easily be the case with a man hungry enough to crush the skull of a helpless drunk—he'd have enough to make a large and ambitious start.

Having nothing specific in mind but his intent to feel his way to the truth, Brazos rode northeast through the dawn light as it grew with a pearly translucence. He crossed a rocky spine of ridge which marked the accepted boundary where Nugget met open range. At the foot of its north slope lay a winter linecamp, a bunkshack and outsheds and holding corral, silent and deserted now that the snows had retreated from the summer range in the high Diablos. Probably it had been headquarters for one of the small outfits that Lambeth had bought out.

From here on, riding deep into pine-belted grass flats, Brazos spooked up a good many fat cattle and their newly dropped calves, and grimly reflected how easily a man could lose all this; one bullet could do it. He climbed through a fringe of foothills and found himself in a deep boxed valley which shouldered tightly against the sudden vault of the peaks, now seeing the ranch headquarters nestled at the head of the valley, almost abutting against a steep timbered slope.

Nearing it, he heard the clean ring of the cook's breakfast triangle. The early sunlight picked out the two-story frame house facing off from the slope, and below it a layout of log outbuildings, old and weather-silvered. These had a square and practical look, and about the whole place there was the feel of a well-run outfit. Every stray scrap of gear was stowed out of the weather, Brazos noted, running his eye over the big barns and solid corrals as he crossed the grassless barn lot.

Following the wagon track that curved around the tack barn, he came suddenly in sight of the long bunkhouse and cookshack. These were connected by a covered runway and set off well below the main house. To his left was a small cabin where a woman stood by the doorway, scattering feed to a flock of chickens. They took squawking and indignant flight as he reined over, touching his hat. *"Buenas dias, senora."*

16

She nodded, a stout middle-aged woman with a roundly pleasant face. "Yes, senor?"

"Who do I see about a job?"

"Ramon Velez, my husband, is foreman here." She turned toward the open door. "Velez!"

"Let a man finish his coffee, eh? Eh, Delores?" A deep voice rumbled gently, and then a stumpy figure of a man stepped out. He was short but broad as a barrel. with a gnarled thickness to his short legs and long arms. His face was like seamed mahogany under a frosty plume of hair. He had the look of authority and something more, a primitive and weathered strength that might have been drawn from the land itself. His rawhide *chivarras* were slick with age, his calico shirt patched and faded, not detracting from his immense earthy dignity. His rumble lowered politely.

"Senor?"

"Looking for work."

Velez took a pack of cornshuck papers from his pocket, freed one and tapped tobacco into it from a reed tube, sizing Brazos all the while. His pale brown eyes were shrewd and merciless in their inspection, not neglecting the ready-worn gun. Brazos, used to that and to some foremen's reaction to the bitter-hard and unthinking insolence of his look, was braced for a turndown. Velez struck a spark into his tinder cord with flint and steel *eslabón*, blew it deftly into flame, and held it to his cigarette. "Let me see your hands."

Brazos held them palms up. Velez grunted, studying callouses and rope scars as he puffed his cigarette alight. "You look to be on a grubline, ranch to ranch."

"Mostly I trap mustangs. Looking for a change."

Velez' eyes glinted. "I swung a loop for the wild ones myself, as a boy." He inhaled smoke deeply and blew it out. "Your name?"

Brazos told him, knowing his trade of mustanger would explain his rough and ragged appearance, and Velez seemed satisfied. "Follow me." They tramped upslope toward the house, Brazos leading his horse. He saw a man step out on the veranda and come unsteadily down the steps, blinking against the raw sunlight.

"Ah. Morning, Ramon."

Velez replied courteously, afterward making introductions. John Lambeth was tall enough, a good six-three, certainly thin, and probably pale under a ruddy tinge of his skin which was not sunburn. His years with Pop Melaven had given Brazos an eye for the florid mottling of a heavy drinker. Lambeth's

17

ash blonde hair made a pale blaze in the sun; his light blue eyes were unnaturally bright, his accent crisp and definite. He wore whipcord breeches and riding boots polished to a high gloss, and, against the morning chill of the high country, a tweedy traveling jacket. The picture was perfect, and yet it jarred; there was a disconcerting innocence to John Lambeth's smile and direct friendly gaze.

"Hullo. Glad to have you on. Fine animal you have there. Take Kane to the cookshack, Ramon, and show him around to the boys, will you?"

Lambeth nodded pleasantly, and as he turned away, stumbled and muttered under his breath. Velez said pointedly, as he and Brazos headed for the bunkhouse, "He is a trusting man, the senor. He likes everyone. It is good he has one to watch out for his interests, to sort out the culls."

"That you?"

"That is me."

"Don't wonder he can't sort his own," Brazos murmured, and Velez turned a hard stare against him. The mayordomo is a good man, and a gentleman. For what a man does to himself, he has his reasons. They are no business of another's. Is your horse used to working brush? Good. He will be useful today. There are plenty of bunks; take your warbag in and take your choice."

The bunkhouse was twenty by sixty, two-roomed, and Brazos passed through the north room with its storage of hide trunks and old gear, and entered the bunkroom. He and Pop Melaven had wintered in many such high country bunkhouses, and this one was typical with its patched old chairs and settee, commode with a warped mirror, central table with its Dutch Almanac and litter of newspapers and magazines, bare well-scrubbed log walls, and seven sets of double bunks, all the bottom ones in use. Brazos tossed his warsack on an empty topbunk and went through the runway with Velez, into the cookshack.

Ten men were seated around the long plank table with two benches flanking either side; they barely glanced up and kept on eating, except for the three of yesterday's encounter. Charley Starr's gaze held sultry and indifferent; he said nothing, and after a lingering stare, returned to his food. So did the cold-eyed man and the chunky one. Brazos thought, as he slid onto a bench alongside a stocky towheaded crewman, that likely they had jumped Pepe Garcia and his sheep without orders, or they'd be quick to mention his part. He had nothing to gain by bringing it up, he decided.

He followed Velez' clockwise introduction of the men: Link Bardine, Red Hollister, Eduardo Chavez, Jigger Kearny, Mose Cruikshank, Fats McEachin—who was of course thin as a rail—and Simon Jack Pima. They had the common stamp of workaday ranchhands, though their ages ranged: Kearny was perhaps a bare eighteen, Mose Cruikshank was a leathery oldtimer. Each man gave a bare word or nod, except Charley Starr; he said politely, "Glad to meet you," his smile white and bland. The ice-eyed Pinto DeVries didn't look up. Chunky Stu Sholto gave Brazos another slitted look, and that was all.

Simon Jack Pima across from him grunted and shook hands, as Velez introduced him: "The Pima, he's the best tracker, best wrangler, best brushpopper in the territory. He will tell you that himself." Simon Jack grunted his agreement. He was a full-blooded tribesman, Brazos guessed, young and lean and wire-muscled, with a barrel chest that filled his faded blue satin shirt. Brazos' place was already set, after the custom of the country, and he turned over his plate and filled it and stolidly ate his second breakfast.

Afterward, fetching up their horses, the crew rode out toward the north basin rim, where an outcropping of badlands shouldered against the peaks. "We are popping the brush there," Velez told Brazos. "There are draws and canyons full of Nugget beef, and they all must be worked out for the tally."

Coming to the first draws and gorges—tortured deep slashes in the weird contortions of massive ridges—Velez split the crew with brusque orders; he let them pair off according to their choosing, each set of partners being assigned a rugged stretch to work out. He said, "Come with me," and led him into a grueling climb of a ridge and a descent of its opposite flank, the stiff brush clawing at their mounts and legs. Brazos had put on his barrel-leg chaps this morning, and was glad of it.

A couple of wild-eyed steers were foraging around a brush-rimmed seep in a bowl behind the ridge, and Velez said, "Take them out." Brazos skirted the pair and hazed them up the ridge flank and across its brow, Velez trailing at a distance as he pushed down past the last draws to the open flats. He did the job with a mechanical competence since he wasn't particularly fond of waddy work. He knew the performance would satisfy Velez, which was all that counted, and turned his first concern to his meeting with John Lambeth.

It had told him little enough, except that the man was

19

fairly green, a steady tippler, and innocuously friendly. That might be total pose, or his heavy drinking might have turned his character inside out. An uneasy conscience might account for either possibility, but for now, until he broke ground for better acquaintance with the crew, Brazos would have to be satisfied to probe delicately for Lambeth's background. Ramon Velez was the most likely to have his boss's confidence, but the foreman's stolid loyalty meant a danger of provoking his suspicions.

Yet, as he and Velez continued to beat the draws and ridges, driving out the scattered ladinos, Brazos found himself falling into an easy, unfeigned kinship with the man. It was kind of coordinated partnership that he and Pop had known, that made any job go smoothly and well. The seed of friendship was here, and Brazos meant to nourish his luck. Velez was his kind of man, and despite his distaste for the notion, he had to consider how he could use this fact.

Toward noon, deep in the northwest ridges, Velez called a break. "We'll have a rest and smoke, eh?" They dismounted and squatted on their heels in a forest of sun-blasted rock; they rolled smokes, and Brazos held the match for both.

"Gracias." Velez tucked away his flint and steel. "An old man likes the old ways too much."

"That's curious," Brazos observed idly. "Understood it was the Montalvo crowd wants to keep the old ways."

Velez' white brows twitched upward. "You mean I'm in strange company?"

"No offense."

"None taken. This must seem curious to an outsider, if he's heard a little. It is not as simple as gringos against Mexes, though that is part of it. Senor Mike of Montalvo is a gringo; on the other hand I grew old with Jay Barstow, helping him build the Nugget. A place becomes part of a man, as much as breathing. When Mr. Lambeth bought out young Tim Barstow, I came with the place. My old ways are my own."

Velez drew on his cigarette, squinting against the smoke as he nodded toward the broken swell of heights to the west. "All that you see yonder, the high summer range, has always been claimed by Montalvo. There are three keys to the basin. You know where it takes its name?"

"Two Troughs?"

Those were two of the keys, said Velez. The Soledad River watered the western range of Montalvo; to this side, the Bison had given life to Nugget and the small Anglo outfits. This, by causing two separate concentrations of growth in each river valley, had given focus to the Mexican-Anglo division, so that the old sharp feelings had been emphasized, rather than softened, with time. The third key was the high grass which Montalvo had never used to capacity; whoever controlled it could grow and expand with the future. By now the low country range was grazed to its limits, and the boundaries of such open grass as remained fixed by understanding. The Anglos might turn covetous eyes toward the high country, but their small outfits, divided by the stubborn independence of Yankee backwoodsmen, would never unite against Montalvo's solid control.

Velez gave a slow and moody nod, studying his cigarette. "All this could change, now one Anglo's bought out half these small outfits. And now Senor Mike O'Brien makes hard talk in public places, calling Senor Lambeth a goddam empire-building Limey and saying that the Irish have taken enough off such sons of bitches. This kind of dare talk alone could set things off, if my patron was not inclined to ignore it. A pity, for these are good men, both." Velez dropped his cigarette stub and ground a heel on it, then eased stiffly to his feet and stretched. "Ahh. Back to work."

He took a step toward his piebald, and then came the high whine of a slug screaming off a rock, followed by the racketing crash of a distant rifle. Rock dust flew inches from Velez' horse, which spun skittishly away as he grabbed at the reins, and afterward bolted away down a small canyon. Velez, cursing, went after him in a stiff run. "Whoa! Hammerhead, *chingado!*" Brazos came off his haunches and lunged after Velez in a half-dive, yelling, "Get down!"

He tackled Velez around the legs and threw him flat, as a second shot whipped above their backs, richocheting. The two men scrambled behind a meager shelter of small rock. Brazos had caught a smudge of powdersmoke along the rim-rock high to the east; the rifleman was laid up above them with a large-caliber weapon.

Velez muttered, his dark face gleaming with sweat, "That was for me, I think."

"Maybe. Fair piece of shooting, but a down angle can throw off a good gunner." Brazos jerked his head to the right. "We move low, we can make that canyon."

Stretched nearly prone on their bellies, hitching themselves along with elbows and dug-in toes, they edged awkwardly across the stony ground behind the shallow barricade of rock. The lip of the coulee where Velez' horse had vanished

21

yawned to their right, and they dropped over the bank and scrambled to the bottom in a moil of dust.

Brazos whistled, and the blue pricked up its ears and trotted toward the coulee. He waited tensely for a shot, but the blue made a safe descent to his side. Velez let out his breath, scrubbing a grimy palm over his brow. "This was close."

Brazos said: "I could swing around and have a look up there."

"No. That's a long way across the open; you would be seen. He'd pot you easy, else be well gone before you reached the rim." Velez scowled. "That rim, she marks the edge of the high range."

"A Montalvo gun, then?"

"I don't like to think so, but that's Montalvo claim." Velez smiled thinly. "Maybe a hothead vaquero of theirs thinks we are ranging too close."

"Didn't seem like any warning shot."

"But I don't think it was ordered. Senor Mike is not a man to fight from ambush. Any man could get up there and shoot a rifle. So long as we don't know who's shooting or why, I think we make no big noise about it—comprendo?"

Brazos shrugged. "Just as you say."

"Bueno. If this marks the start of trouble, more will come. If not, we don't want a fuss of Nugget's making to set it off. Now we'll follow the canyon and find my horse."

CHAPTER THREE

BRAZOS WAS THE FIRST to finish supper and return to the bunkhouse, where he lay on his bunk and smoked his after-supper cigarette and stared at the ceiling. He had a fair opening to Velez' confidence by which he could dig deeper, given time. For now he let his thoughts idly veer to this morning's deadfall. There had been speculation among the crew about the shots they'd heard, and old Mose Cruikshank had opined that the rifle had been a deep-voiced Sharps. Velez had blandly asked if anyone had seen anything back in the breaks, and they had agreed to a man that they hadn't.

A buffalo gun, Brazos mused, *now that's something.* With his casual attention to details, he'd noted that of the crew only Stu Sholto carried a .50 Sharps in his saddle boot. It was a cumbersome weapon made for a hunter in an all-day stand, designed by its deep-muted boom not to spook game hards. A squat bull of a man like Sholto could handle its shattering power, but a horseback man if he packed a rifle at all usually favored a stubby carbine.

When you thought about it, there was a surefire puzzle to the way those three, Charley Starr and Pinto DeVries and Sholto, hung together. A lonely country made strange partners, but the only thing that trio seemed to have in common was an indefinable something that set them off from the others. Charley Starr had the long catty build of a range-rider, but his disciplined speech and manner were those of an educated man, his slight lisp smothering any regional accent. Easier to assess the Texan DeVries with his chill stare and gaunt hungry look: his gun was his stock in trade. Brazos had seen enough like him in trail town and mining camp, where they gravitated to trouble like iron filings to a magnet. In a different way the same could be said of Stu Sholto, all brutal beef and shallow wit, who could find a raw pleasure in dragging a Mexican sheepman on a rope.

Thinking about it prompted a more-or-less idle impulse which, since he was alone in the bunkroom, Brazos followed up. He dropped off the bunk and crossed the room to

23

Sholto's gear stacked by the foot of his bunk. He picked up the Sharps and opened the breech, extracting the four-inch shell seated there. He sniffed the chamber, and his first thought caught on a tight blank as a sound by the open door pulled him around. Charley Starr was leaning there, his wide bland face and hooded eyes without expression. "I'd call that playing hell, Red, prying in another man's possibles."

Brazos said nothing, and Starr glanced over his shoulder and said, "Stu," afterward stepping on into the room. The rest of the crew filed in then, picking their teeth and passing idle talk, which broke off as they saw Brazos still holding the rifle. Sholto himself hauled up short, a dull anger flickering in his face, and Brazos grinned at him. "Had cause to fire this today, did you?"

It was Charley Starr who answered, with a faintly quizzical politeness. "Late yesterday. What of it?"

Brazos set the rifle on the bunk, a slow insolence hardening in his eyes. "You tell me."

Starr lifted one shoulder in a mild shrug. "Stu took a shot at a deer. We're all sick of beef, figured Coosie could spoil some venison for a change."

The crew exchanged curious glances, and now old Mose Cruikshank put in stolidly, "Well, like he says, son, what of it?"

"Maybe nothing," Brazos began, and then out of the tail of his eye caught the sudden shift of Sholto's bulk. And spun toward him in time to catch the full, meaty sledge of the man's fist.

Black light exploded in Brazos' head as he backpedaled, slamming into the wall. He heard the grunt of his own driven breath, and felt his knees give way and stiffened them instinctively; he doggedly shook his head to clear it. Dimly he heard Sholto rumble, "You got a big nose, boy. Don't like no man fooling with my gun," and shook his head again, the room coming into watery focus now. Sholto's short massive form bulked before him, feet planted wide, his fist pulling back. In the last instant Brazos bent his knees and dropped his head.

Sholto's hand crashed into the wall; he gave an agonized bellow. Brazos' head was still ringing, but he braced his palms against the wall and heaved forward, butting Sholto in the chest. It was like trying to buck a rock wall, and with a savage grunt now, Sholto stepped away, sweeping his good fist in a backhand cuff. It sent Brazos kiting into the table. In the jarring pain of it he somehow kept his feet, fumbling

24

around the edge of the table as he moved backward. Sholto heaved after him, cuddling his hurt hand to his chest, his thick face twisted in a brutal grimace of fury.

Brazos kept moving to keep the table between himself and the hulking man till the groggy numbness washed away. He could see again, and there was tearing pain in his right ear where Sholto's fist had angled viciously across the side of his face. The crew had pulled back to the walls, and it was the two of them alone; he had a fleeting look at the bland pleasure in Charley Starr's face, and thought, *first things first*, and put all his attention on Sholto. He'd halted, his small eyes squinted in pain as held his bleeding hand by the wrist, slowly working his hairy fingers. "Ain't broke," he rumbled, "but you're sure-hell gonna get stomped, little man."

Brazos had reached the foot of the table, and his quick glance found the heavy lamp toward this end. Sholto was moving after him now, and then a feral growl broke in his chest and he lunged headlong. Brazos stepped sideways and scooped up the lamp, and as Sholto bulled past, swung it full-armed and brought it crashing against the man's neck.

The weighted base caught Sholto under the right ear, and he went on past, his bullet head striking a bunk sideboard with an impact that shook the building. He bounced, or seemed to, and his knees hinged; he folded to the floor without a sound. He lay in a face-down sprawl, runnels of coal oil streaking his hair and neck and shirt.

Brazos braced his palms against the table, taking back his breath, then bent to pick up the lamp. It was unbroken, and he set it gently on the table, letting his stare lock Charley Starr's with open challenge.

"What is this racket?" Ramon Velez came into the room at a stiff angry stride. His mustaches twitched to the startled tightening of his lips, his slow glance shuttling from Sholto's prone form to Brazos. "You hit him?"

"As hard as I could," Brazos said thinly. "Found his Sharps was shot off recent, and he didn't like it."

"So," Velez frowned. "That could be interesting." The men were eying him with curious expectancy, and briefly then he explained about the deadfall this morning. "I didn't want this noised about, but maybe that was unwise. Maybe."

"Now," Charley Starr said wonderingly, "why should Stu do that? You're wrong, Ramon, if—"

"You were with him all day, eh, Charley."

"Surest thing you know. As I told this Kane fellow, Stu

shot at a mule buck yesterday. Hell, Ramon, we heard those shots today too."

"You told me," Brazos said. "Now tell him about that Mexican kid you gave a Dutch ride."

Velez had moved over to pick up Sholto's Sharps and sniff the breech, and he lowered it frowning. "What is that?"

"DeVries ran off this Mex boy's sheep yesterday and Sholto dragged him on a rope. Starr gave the order. I heard it and I saw it, coming off the pass." His hard stare riveted Charley Starr's. "It's your three to my one, so call me a liar. Go ahead."

He swung out from the table, putting his right hand in the clear, and now Charley Starr lifted his hands with a placating good humor. "Well, you do go with that hair. Sure, we roughed that young fellow up. He was over the line, Ramon."

"You're a liar," Brazos said flatly. "It was public domain."

"This is hard talk, and I think enough of it," Velez said with a brittle authority. "How do you know this?"

"The boy told me. Pepe Garcia."

Velez frowned. "I know Pepe, he's a good boy." Several of the men shuffled restlessly, and he gave a dry nod. "The pepperbellies stick together, you're thinking?"

Young Eduardo Chavez' eyes glinted darkly. "A man who thinks that, he should speak out."

Old Mose Cruikshank tongued his tobacco into the pouch of a whiskered cheek, saying meagerly, "Reckon no takers. You was saying, Ramon?"

"I am saying nobody's sure of the lines," Velez said curtly. "Maybe it was a mistake, yours or Pepe's. Just so there's not another."

Charley Starr stirred his shoulders in a bare shrug. "You're the boss. Possibly we were hasty. But sheep, even a handful, on cattle grass . . . well, you're a cowman, Ramon."

Brazos murmured, "And you?"

"Enough hard talk, I said. Maybe we should step outside." Velez nodded at the sprawled hulk of Sholto, said, "Throw some water on him," and went out the door, Brazos following. His mashed earlobe, bleeding on his shirt now, throbbed to bitter life in the cooling twilight. A little way from the bunkhouse Velez halted and, Brazos thought wryly, *Now you've done it, and it's pick up your time.* But Velez only growled, "My woman will look at that ear. Come along."

In Velez' cabin, Brazos sat at the table while Delores Velez tilted his head to the light, inspecting his ear with a stormy frown. "Men, fighting like dogs. Look at the soft part

26

of the ear, nearly torn off. I will have to sew it." Clucking angrily, she bustled to draw water and set it on the stove.

Velez went to a cabinet and took out a demijohn and a tin cup. He filled the cup and handed it to Brazos, saying with no heat, "So. You know Sholto didn't shoot at a deer, eh?"

"No," Brazos said coldly. "Just pretty damn' sure. So are you, or you'd cuss me out for a hardnose and send me packing."

Velez smiled, rubbing his chin. "You're a hardnose, all right. I ask, can you prove any of that?"

Brazos had the irritable feel of cross-currents he didn't understand. "I don't need to. Neither do you. Hire and fire here, don't you? Tell 'em to slope it."

Velez swung out a chair and straddled it, folding his arms on its back. "Listen, I am not quite a fool. This Starr—and Pinto and Stu only follow his lead—has put a bad smell in my nose since he came on. Still, so long as they don't dog their work, so long as I can't prove what I think, can I fire them and keep the respect of my men?"

Delores had brought strips of cloth and a basin of hot water to the table; she bathed Brazos' torn ear, her fingers gentle and her voice tart: "Men, you are all such big men. You are like little boys. *Es barbaridad.*"

"Be still, woman. You see this, Brazos?"

Having lived totally in a man's world since he was ten, he had to concede the bleak truth behind Velez' words. But he said stubbornly, "Suppose it touches the ranch?"

"That's different; you're thinking of yesterday. It might have been very bad if you had not helped Pepe, but you did. As I said, the boundary lines are not clear, and before this, riders have roughed up sheepmen. I did not hire those three; Senor Lambeth did, and he would want a strong reason to discharge them. To stop more such trouble and any such deadfall as they may have tried for me today—which we don't surely know—is as easy as breaking them apart at work is going to be—assigning others to work with each. Now drink deep, so Delores can sew your ear."

"I sew nothing," she said flatly, "till you say what this is about." The concern deepened in her round face as Velez told her, but she only sighed and shook her head then. "Do you wonder that I worry for such a man? He has his honor and his pride, and too little fear."

She produced a needle and some silken thread, and Brazos took the pale liquor in a swallow, his eyes watering with the

27

white fire of it. He held his breath, hands clamped around his knees, as Delores swiftly and deftly pierced his ear. "Two stitches, I think. There."

After Velez had refilled his cup and he'd drunk again, Brazos said, "I must be missing something. What's special about Starr and his pair of jokers?"

"This might be obvious," Velez said with a dour smile. "I sized these three when they drifted in a couple weeks back looking for rider's jobs. More likely it's that they heard of the trouble brewing here, and figured in a lefthanded way to hire out their guns. I would have told the senor so, but Mrs. Lambeth . . ."

Brazos' quick lift of head jarred Delores' fingers as she bandaged his ear. "He has a wife?"

"That woman," Delores muttered acidly. "Sit still, senor!"

"Watch your tongue," Velez said severely. "She's the patron's wife."

"Hah. That one, I think I know what she is."

Velez frowned darkly, but looked again at Brazos. "Mrs. Lambeth headed me off, saying these men looked right to handle anything that Montalvo might start. It was my thought, though I didn't say so, that hiring such men would ask for trouble. At first maybe Senor Lambeth had the same thought, but . . . eh, his senora has a very convincing way."

Delores gave a derisive sniff. "She has this, Velez, certainly. With men. What fools you all are."

"Yes, and what a cross we all bear in woman's wagging tongue. So they were hired, and I think it will take much to show the Lambeths this was a mistake." He hesitated, then tapped the table with a blunt forefinger. "I tell you this in confidence, comprendo? I think Mrs. Lambeth may have promised Charley the foreman's place if he hired on. She is very sure that we need a fighting force to match Montalvo—men who can handle guns more than cows."

"And," Delores sniffed, "she is working hard on the senor to get it."

"Perhaps, but they are both greenhorns and don't know better. Why Charley should want my job so bad is not clear, but after this fuss tonight, I think I'll watch him ver' close."

Delores carried the basin of dirty water outside with a brusque nod to Brazos' "Gracias." He felt of the bulky bandage on his ear, saying idly, "She came here with her husband?"

Velez gave him a sharp look. "Yes. Mrs. Lambeth is in Soledad now. She is due back tomorrow, on the train. Maybe

28

you will meet her then." He stood, walked to the water bucket and scooped up a dipperful of water. He drank, his profile like a wooden Toltec mask, and Brazos knew that something in his words or manner was bothering Velez. But he thought stubbornly, *Hell, you got to find out sometime.*

"They're English, I reckon?"

Velez dropped the dipper in the bucket, eying him thoughtfully as if making up his mind. Then he came back to the table. "No. Senor Lambeth is of a wealthy New York family. He got his learning in England, at places called Rugby and Oxford. Later, he was a surveyor for the government here in the West. It was then, he said, he decided he would ranch here one day. It was after he met and married his senora in New Orleans, that he came back to the territory and bought up the outfits here in Two Troughs." A dry pause. "That is all he told me."

Brazos said, "That so," as he smothered a yawn. But Velez' explanation had left him with an irritated bafflement, and he thought, *All right, say he lied to Velez about his past. Maybe, but go careful.* He picked up his hat and stood. "Getting late, and a long day tomorrow. Ma'am, thank you again."

"Senor, Velez is a very foolish husband. Thank me by watching him well, on the range."

"Women," grunted Velez. "Buenas noches."

CHAPTER FOUR

AFTER BREAKFAST the crew assembled at the corral to wait for Velez and the day's orders. The strain of last night's incident was on their minds, and there was little talk. Brazos leaned at his ease against the fence and rolled a smoke, giving Stu Sholto a studied disregard. This morning the whole side of Sholto's beefy neck was swollen and discolored. Brazos' own jaw ached steadily and had given him trouble eating, and now and then his stitched ear caught a sharp twinge. Sholto's chunky build belied its massive underquilting of muscle; he'd nearly disabled Brazos with two blows. After lighting his cigarette, Brazos made an insolent point of tossing the dead match at Sholto's boots.

Sholto shifted his feet, bridling ominously, and Charley Starr gave him a warning look. Pinto DeVries stood hipshot, his arms folded, never taking his icy stare off the horse-trapper. The lines were drawn here and the others knew it, and had no part of it.

Presently Velez tramped out of his house. told them good morning, and gave his orders. True to his word, he broke up Charley Starr and company. Sholto would work over to the south line with Jigger Kearny; DeVries would brush-comb with Link Bardine over northeast, and the rest of them would continue to pop the north breaks. While the men were saddling, John Lambeth strode up. He had a liverish and sickly look, and hungover as he was, must have forced himself out of bed.

"Good morning, senor," Velez said courteously. "There is something?"

"Quite. Er . . . wondered if one of you might volunteer to drive Mrs. Lambeth from the station? Her train should be in this morning."

Brazos hesitated only a moment. "I will." He had barely spoken, he noted, ahead of Charley Starr, who closed his mouth now. His face was not pleasant, and Brazos thought, *Now that touched a raw spot—wonder why.*

Lambeth peered at him. "Hullo. Oh, Kane. Yes, come along;

30

I'll show you the rig." His hesitation in placing the man he'd hired yesterday was not surprising; he'd been rolling then and he had probably kept it up all day. Brazos was aware of Velez' shrewdly curious glance at him, but the foreman said nothing.

After putting his saddle away, he joined Lambeth by the carriage shed, which was crowded with all kinds of rigs from a broken-down surrey to an ancient ore wagon with the wheels missing. Lambeth lightly slapped the seat of a spring wagon. "She hates the blasted ride coming and going—road to Diablo's not graded worth a damn. And not a rig on the place worth a dash-dash, but this one has the best springs. Use the two bays—well-gaited brutes." He smiled with a faint embarrassment. "Should ride in myself. Bit under the weather though. Bloke ought to learn better, eh? Save his sozzling for Saturday nights."

There was something wistful in this confiding attempt at friendliness, and Brazos had the odd, sudden impression that John Lambeth was a lonely man. The irritation it brought hardened his voice: "How will I know her?"

"Of course, forgot you're new." An indrawn squint touched Lambeth's gaze. "Small, blonde, quite fetching if I do say so. And the voice of course. Southern, you know." He paused with the air of a man wanting to convey more, shrugged and smiled. "Hard to miss Lila Mae. Well, you'd better get along—you'll be rather early, but she objects strenuously to being kept waiting."

Thoughtfully Brazos watched him walk, somewhat unsteadily, back toward the house. It was natural to dovetail the man's lonely air into Delores Velez' harsh judgment of his wife. With the thought, a dark anger touched Brazos. *Don't go soft in the head.* Either Lambeth was what he 'claimed to be, or a monument of bland deceit. It would be too easy to be drawn by his warm likeableness, or turning the coin over, to resenting his easy gall if you got thinking it was that. A meeting with his wife might tell more, but Brazos' first reason for a trip to the Two Troughs county seat was to put a question to the local sheriff, the man most likely to have information on the kind of man he sought.

He had no difficulty singling out the matched copperbottom bays, special-gaited for teamwork. When he had them harnessed and hitched, he mounted the wagon and clucked them into a brisk clip on the town road. It cut through a notch downvalley and afterward followed a straight trace across fairly open country, sparsely grassed and tree-dotted. He had

31

a good view of the fallaway terraces to the northeast, where Montalvo lay. The gently ridge-broken plains swept upward to the higher terraces of what he supposed was the disputed high range.

There was, he reflected, a kind of inevitable trend where men and power were concerned: the scarred-muzzled old dog growling over his bone, the young pup driven to test his new muscles. Greed was only instinct when you came down to it —the ancient and irrational voice of survival. *Survival of the fittest.* He'd had a book on the subject by a British scientist named Huxley, which Pop Melaven had traded off to a whiskey drummer for a batch of miniature sample bottles.

Musing without much real cynicism in the drowsy splendor of the morning, Brazos presently crossed the thaw-swollen rush of the Bison, and from here the land climbed steadily toward the gentle barren divide that partitioned the two trough-shaped river valleys. Shortly after crossing it, he clucked the team over a bald hill and saw Diablo below. It was a backcountry town—three blocks of weathered false fronts, wooden overhangs, and sagging tie-racks; it made a dark rough blend with the surrounding country, softly green with high-grass spring. The main roads from the north and the east forked to one on the hill and switchbacked off it, and became a mud-channeled main street, trampled to its spring mire by a traffic of wheels, hoofs and boots.

Brazos came into the town from its east end, crossed the tracks and came at once to the squat frame building which housed jail and sheriff's office, with its faded legend over the entrance. He pulled up at the rack, came off the wagon, and went in without knocking. He introduced himself, shook hands with Sheriff Keogh and Ralph Means, the watery-eyed and chinless jailor, and slacked into a vacant barrel chair.

"What can I do for you?"

Liam Keogh's tone was neutral, while he sized his visitor with flinty gray eyes. He was a tall weedy Texan in his forties with a drooping sorrel mustache that deepened the mournful aloofness of his long face. Brazos assessed him as a man shy on imagination, but not experience; he would handle any job he knew with a hard, no-nonsense competence.

After barely stating that he was looking for a man, he made his description detailed and thorough. Keogh's unblinking stare sharpened. "Pretty tight description. Only man might fill it is John Lambeth, owner of Nugget."

"I know," Brazos said dryly. "I hired on there."

"Did you now?" Keogh was sitting with elbows on his desk,

fingers steepled lightly; he lowered them to the desk and picked up a pencil, his eyes not moving. "Not your man, I reckon, or you wouldn't be here."

"Hard to say. Wondered if you'd have a flyer that might fit him."

"He's wanted, then? You a federal man?"

"No."

"Bounty hunter?"

"No." Brazos had held only a thin hope that he might skirt his reason for inquiry; there would be no shunting it aside with this lawman. He made his explanation meager, and without a word Keogh reached in a drawer and pulled out a sheaf of papers and tossed them on the desk. Brazos hitched his chair up and leafed through the wanted notices, and handed them back with a shake of his head and the wry thought: *Wasted time, and now come the questions.*

Keogh steepled his fingers again. "Good reason to find this man, if what you say is fact. Maybe you're the man to find him, seeing you got nothing better to do. Seeing he's got your money, too."

Brazos was silent to the question implied but unsaid, and Keogh picked up the pencil and tapped it gently against his crossed knee. "Like I say, you have your look around. Find him, you let me know. I'll take him in and hold him, same for the money if he has it, and check back on your story. If it fits, you should get your money back."

Brazos held a stubborn silence, and now Keogh rose and came around his desk, set his fists on it and leaned over Brazos. "You listen, Red. There's one man in Two Troughs country settles for the law, and it ain't you." The edge of his voice blunted slightly. "Hell, I know how a man feels. Killed a man in Texas who wronged my sister. Your age then, or less. That was a wide-open time, no law in hundreds of miles, but I thought plenty on it later. Right's right and wrong's wrong."

Brazos said softly, "And who decides?"

"Here, I do."

"Know what citizen's arrest is?" Brazos looked up as he spoke, and Keogh gave a narrow-eyed nod. Brazos pushed to his feet, looping a thumb in his belt; his temper became reflected in the cold insolence of his grin. "With due cause, as I read it, a private citizen can make his own arrest. Say there's no law on the spot to bring a man down. Say he breaks, too. This fellow—I figure he'll break."

"And then he's dead."

33

"I say that? He'll get fetched up in one hell of a hurry."
Brazos started toward the door grinning, and the sheriff's
sharp question brought him up there.

"One thing, son. This old fellow who raised you, the one
you want to settle for. What you reckon he'd say about
that?"

"What he never said when he was alive, for sure. Amen.
Just that, sheriff." He touched his hat politely, and went out,
his grin fading to a residue of grim amusement. He had made
a halfway bluff, but it left the sheriff's hands neatly tied, or
so it seemed—at least Keogh hadn't pushed his first implied
threat. Maybe he wanted to consult a lawyer first.

When you can't lick 'em, join 'em, Brazos thought, as he
quartered across toward the general merchandise store. But
his real thoughts were sober with the deadly promise he'd
made the dead old drunk who had been as much father and
mentor as he'd known for half his green years. Memory softened the harsh edges; the good remained, and there had been
too much of it, too long close to him, to deserve a brutal death
in a nameless alley.

There were also twelve thousand dollars for which he had
sweated blood for a year, and he wasn't about to sneeze that
lightly away either. Flat broke after Pop's death, he'd been
determined to pay off his Mexican wranglers and had ridden a
hundred miles to get the money from an old debtor of his,
practically having to force it from him at gunpoint. He'd always been too free and easy with money, but that time was
past, and the stolen twelve thousand was coming out of someone, or out of someone's hide.

Stepping into the spicy gloom of the store, he named his
needs to the wizened clerk: a new outfit of halfboots, denim
pants and two calico shirts. He changed in the store room at
the back after learning there was no barber shop with bath
in town, discarded his ragged, filthy clothes and seam-broken
boots in an empty box, clamped on the battered comfort of
his old slouch hat, and sought the street again.

He drove the wagon down to the depot, hauled up on the
cinder apron, and nodded to the station agent's sharp "Hoddy"
as the old man came out to the siding, peering testily at his
watch. Brazos thumbed out his makings as the distant shriek
of the locomotive drifted down the tracks; he was deeply enjoying the acrid bite of his first smoke for the day as the train
jolted and coupling-crashed to a halt. The brakeman dropped
off a forward car, gave the bitter old agent a phlegmatic
hello, and began handing down pieces of luggage.

The conductor assisted a woman from the passenger coach; she murmured a gentle thank you and looked around, her gaze lighting at once on Brazos. "Are you from Nugget?"

He touched a finger to his hat, said, "Yes'm," tossed away his smoke and stepped down. She gave him a small hand, her smile quick and bright. "Reckon you're new. I'm Lila Mae Lambeth."

Brazos told his name, his regard of her careful and almost wary. She was rounded and small in a dust-wrinkled traveling suit; her face was like a china doll's, fragile and lovely, her honey-tinted curls peeping demurely from a pale green bonnet that matched her eyes. The pout of her lips made her look very young, but the faint etching of lines at the corners of her eyes placed her in perhaps her late twenties. Brazos had never met a rich man's kind of woman, but he had peopled that world with gracious ladies, and John Lambeth's wife surely seemed to fit her place.

"I declare," she murmured. "Always good to hear a real Southern voice this far north. I'm surely tired, Mr. Kane, and I won't mind if we hustle going back."

Brazos loaded her baggage, mostly packages which felt like dress goods, into the wagon bed. Afterward he assisted her to the seat, clucked the team into motion and swung briskly onto the east road. Lila Mae Lambeth kept up a gay, pleasant chatter that was more lightheaded than his taste ran, and considering the heap of frothy packages in the wagon bed he guessed that her visit to Soledad had been wholly a shopping spree. Still she seemed a likely match for the dude Lambeth, and it deepened the puzzle of the man's drinking. Lambeth was an unhappy man, and it was hard to see why. Young, rich, with a beautiful wife, he should be the envy of nearly any man.

A bad conscience might be the answer, but Brazos was getting impatient with odd guesses about Lambeth. A wanted man, particularly if he established a new life and identity, would destroy the concrete details of his past, but there was always the chance that out of sentiment he'd overlook an item or two. Brazos had reconnoitered the house last night, before turning in, to place the ranch office. Tonight, if after a search of John Lambeth's papers and possessions, he found nothing . . . somehow he didn't want to think beyond that.

The road dropped now onto a desolate flat flanked to the south by a swatch of badlands. A jag of scrubby cattle was moving out of a nearby draw, hazed at loose point by two riders. The dust boiling up on a whiplash of wind made a dim

35

bulky shape of the rider in the drag. Noting that the cattle would shortly quarter across the road ahead of the wagon, Brazos halted the team.

"Go on," Lila Mae said a trifle sharply.

"Cattle crossing got the right of way, ma'am."

As the bunch moved onto the road, the drag rider wheeled out his mount, shading his eyes with his hand; he bawled an order. The other two gently crowded the lead steers, and the bunch moved to a halt. The dragman put his horse toward the wagon. Brazos had guessed that these brushpoppers were Montalvo men working out their south-ranging culls, and he made another guess about this big Anglo who bossed them.

Mike O'Brien careened his shaggy little cutter to a stop. There was a colorful dash to his *taja* leggings and embroidered *charro* jacket discolored by dust and old stains, and a wry gallantry to his half-bow. In saddle, the thick girth of his trunk and shoulders offset his height. A black Spanish hat was shoved back on his full shock of iron-gray hair, and his wide sunboiled face was full of a weathered toughness tempered by easy humor. His teeth bared in a chalky grin, a twisted cheroot tilted jauntily between them.

"Ah, Mrs. Lambeth it is. You wouldn't be thinking to drive through us, my dear?"

"Where I'm from, Mr. O'Brien, white folks generally go first. Niggers or greasers, it's one to me."

The words were somehow ugly, belying the facile sweetness of her tone, and it startled Brazos. Not that her sentiment was uncommon, but he wouldn't have expected it so blatantly voiced by a quality lady.

Mike O'Brien threw back his head with a hearty roar. "Ah, there's a little lady; claws under the velvet." He shuttled his sparkling gray eyes to Brazos. "You'd be new with this petticoat outfit?"

"Hired on yesterday."

"You have a look about you, and it's not a winning one. John Lambeth has hired on some mean ones of late, and I'm thinking you're another." O'Brien took his cheroot from his mouth, stabbed it gently at the air. "It points that Lambeth is stoking up a fine fire that may roast him, and a smart lad won't stay around to get his fingers burned."

"I got no part of that."

"There'll be no middle ground if it comes, mark that."

Lila Mae said impatiently, "Will you please get those cows on?"

"Now," O'Brien grinned around his cheroot, "why should I? They're due a rest."

Brazos grinned back. "We're not."

O'Brien curbed his fiddlefooting horse and revolved his cheroot in his teeth, studying Brazos some more. "You may be a mal hombre, Mr. Middleman, but don't play the bucko lad with me."

"Depends on you." Brazos' cold stare moved to the two vaqueros, as they quietly sidled their horses up. "Any crowding here, you'll start it. You may not finish it."

O'Brien barked an order over his shoulder; the pair pulled back to flanking places and prodded the herd. As the bunch shifted on, O'Brien threw his cheroot away with a savage abruptness. "That was fair enough, my lad, but I don't like your face. If I ever catch a smell of you across my line, you're dead." He turned the cutter on a rough rein and moved off with the drag, and Brazos clucked the team up.

Lila Mae gave him a quizzical sideglance. "My, bet you got a dash of vinegar for just about everyone."

"No'm. Only happens they ask for it."

"Why, that's fine." Her soft laugh was musical. "Man with all that vinegar can be useful, provided he throws it the right way."

CHAPTER FIVE

LILA MAE LAMBETH wondered idly, studying her image in her full-length mirror, why you had to lose the means to obtain nice things before you could truly appreciate them. She patted her shining curls, gave a little fillip to the frothy collar of her gown, pinched her cheeks to bring color, and smiling her satisfaction, half-spanned her narrow waist with her palms. A good man could still span it completely, and she decided that she was holding up nicely at thirty-two. Pale green matched her eyes and flattered her coloring, and the tight bodice delicately flaunted her bosom and erect small shoulders.

She passed for twenty-six, and that would do for poor old John, she thought with humorous contempt. But a discerning man—and she frowned slightly—would notice the telltale etchings at the corners of eyes and mouth. She touched them with a light brooding gesture; even soft lamplight and half-shadow did not entirely erase them. She had to be more sparing with smiles and frowns, always useful but prone to wrinkling. She smiled very slightly, and thought she liked the effect.

Lila Mae smoothed her hands over her skirt, enjoying rustle of fresh crinoline with the greedy savor of a little girl. How good to have such things again, and she did have to congratulate herself on that matter . . .

She had been on the lookout for just such a windfall when she had invested the scrimped savings of a less respectable occupation into developing a large and fashionable dress-makers' shop in New Orleans. By cultivating the friendship and confidence of her affluent customers, she had received invitations to their houses, and finally to a gala ball for which she had spent a week preparing a gown. There had been an abundance of young bloods from the old Creole families and the newer Yankee merchant class. She had gloried in that evening, at the same time bending every wile a beautiful woman could command to a fixed goal in her mind. From the

38

moment she was introduced to young John Lambeth, gentleman of leisure, her mind was made up.

At first his backward shyness had seemed almost a pose; the man was as ignorant and inept with a woman as any stuttering, red-eared trailhand, the more puzzling because he was an educated and well-traveled man. But the reason was soon clear. He was an only son with no sisters; his mother had died when he was two, and his wealthy father, determined to raise no mollycoddle son, had subjected him totally to men's company and recreations—habit more deeply rooted by John's years of study in the womanless world of English schools. His work as surveyor had taken him into little-inhabited areas where women were few and far between. Only after his father's recent death had he begun to enjoy the profligate social life of a rich man's heir, and Lila Mae had caught him at the outset.

She did not share John's taste for rough and wild places, having had a fill of the brawling frontier before coming to New Orleans, but she had nevertheless encouraged his dream of ranching in the West. Her own past had left Lila Mae with a deeply submerged fear of poverty, and marrying into wealth was a sure escape. But her real ambition dovetailed into her husband's dream. The Western fortunes were built on cattle and land, and land was power; her past had taught her that too. Her lodestar was a picture of herself as mistress of a feudal domain where her snap of a finger was law. And the lodestar had become an obsession.

Again the unconscious frown marred Lila Mae's forehead as, leaving her room now, she walked to the parlor with a crisp rustle of skirts. She had worked on John with every time-worn trick at her command, and still was making no headway against the high principles instilled by his schooling and class upbringing. He had lived among rough men and was no stranger to danger and violence—he was surely no coward—and he was pathetically pliant in the hands of a knowledgeable woman. Yet she could smile or frown, wheedle or threaten, give or withhold, and never dent that infuriating damned fairmindedness of his.

Lila Mae smoothed her face to sweet composure as she entered the parlor, but circled it with a distasteful glance. The whole room was an extension of the late owner's blunt uncurried personality. It was pine-floored, with a great flagstone fireplace at each end, and the hand-hewn wall timbers were hung with bright Navajo blankets, hunting trophies and ancient rifles and pistols. The furniture was comfortably battered and scarred, the leather settee and armchairs seam-sprung. But time enough, with her first concern settled, to rectify unpleasant details.

John Lambeth was slacked in his armchair by the east fire-place, brooding into its cheerful blaze. His chin was sunk on his chest, as he turned an empty glass between his fingers. Lila Mae's nostrils flared with faint disgust; his drinking was worsening, and obviously he'd stayed in a whiskey stupor during the three days of her absence.

She came up beside him and playfully ruffled his hair, and he looked up quickly, with a bleary hesitance. In trying to wear down his resistance, she had exhibited a range of capricious behavior that John, she knew, put down to a moody unpredictability. So far, though, her calculated extremes of mood had only driven him into sloughs of bewildered misery which he dulled with drink—for through it all, John Lambeth had remained hopelessly, helplessly in love with her.

She murmured now, brushing her lips to his, "How's my old darlin' been?"

His uncertainty dissolved and he reached for her hungrily. She stepped away with a demure laugh, taking his glass, then moved to the sideboard to refill it. He was still fairly sober, and impatient as she was with her old strategy, Lila Mae decided to press it once more.

"Honey, I do wish you'd get rid of that Velez—"

"Confound it, do you have to start that again?"

There was a harried sharpness in the words, and she widened her eyes to startled hurt, touching her scented kerchief to her lips. "Declare, Mr. Lambeth, you needn't shout."

He was instantly contrite. "I'm sorry—blast it. It's the liquor."

Lila Mae gave a sniff and a toss of her curls. "Well, there's only one person can help *that*."

"Yes," he said wearily, and returned to his chair. He hunched forward, leaned an elbow on his knee and scrubbed his hand slowly over his face. "Perhaps we should discuss the matter, though where it will get us . . ."

"Honey, look." She came to his chair and knelt, laying a hand on his knee. "It's just as simple can be. Sooner or later that O'Brien is going to move; just a question of time till he's ready. And we're sitting around all unprepared till he catches us unawares—"

"My dear," Lambeth broke in exasperatedly, "there is no evidence that O'Brien intends anything of the sort."

"Oh, there never is." A brittle shine filled Lila Mae's green eyes. "That's how my daddy thought when the Yankee Army came through Georgia. All those stories of Yankee atrocities were just a lot of war propaganda, he said; General Billy Sherman was a gentleman who'd abide by the rules of civilized warfare. A civilized conquering army simply did not wage war on civilians. So we didn't prepare. And General Billy Sherman's foragers overran our plantation and burned what they couldn't carry off. We could have armed the slaves; even the women and children in our family would have taken up guns. He lost his life trying to defend his house. They shot him like a dog in his own parlor. Because he started his fight a mite late, you see."

The bitter hate she could not keep from her voice was genuine, and even the story was substantially true. Only her father had been a dirt-poor sharecropper on a neighboring tenant farm, and the plantation owner's daughter had been another girl of her age, the object of her hateful envy. Time and again over the years, prowling the grounds of that fine place to spy on the girl's activities, she had been chased off by their fat sleek Negro servants. *Git out o' here, you no 'count po' trash.* If she lived to be a hundred . . .

She looked down at her fist crushing the folds of her fine skirt, and unclenched it, smoothing the material with a quick glance at John. He was staring into his glass, saying, "I know. You've told me all this, and I understand your feelings. But that was war, Lila Mae. You can't impose an entirely different set of circumstances on the situation here. To build up for a fight that may never come will only provoke worse tension. And there's nothing to warrant that O'Brien will—"

"Why, he's been bragging all over the country what he'll do!"

"My dear, look at the facts. O'Brien is not shy one square foot of land, even open range, that he didn't possess before we came. Of course, our buying up so much land and building a good-sized outfit has made him naturally suspicious; he fears that we may be flexing our muscles to take more. But the gist of his loud talk, as I understand it, is we had better give him no concrete cause for concern."

She broke in angrily, telling of today's encounter on the road. "Seems to me that shows what sort of man he is. He'd have stalled us there long as it pleased him, if not for Mr. Kane. And the things he said!"

Lambeth shifted uneasily. "Oh, come now, Lila Mae. Hardly sounds as bad as all that."

She rose swiftly, with a hiss of starched petticoats. "A man insults your wife, and you pass it off like nothing."

"Very well," he said tiredly. "What shall I do?"

"Make ready. Just that. Get rid of that plodding old foreman and put in a younger man. Hire on some men who won't shy at fighting for their outfit, if necessary."

"We have at least three of those," he said dryly. "I agreed to hiring Starr, DeVries and Sholto because three rough and ready crewmen hardly constitute a provocation—and that only to please you. But three more could make all the difference—"

"Between readiness and getting caught cold, yes!"

"—and a foreman of that stripe would certainly provoke trouble," Lambeth went on patiently. "I take it that you still have Charley Starr in mind?"

"Why not? Unless I'm mistaken, the man's intelligent, competent, and a natural leader."

"And a fairly proddy chap, I should think, given the right situation." Lambeth shook his head stubbornly. "No. I'm sorry, my dear, but no. Velez has shown competence, and more—loyalty. You can't buy or sell that. I can hardly show less to him." He shook his head bitterly. "I don't understand. It wasn't like this between us at first; now for a reason I can't grasp it's gone bad. Have I failed you, somehow? I promised you the best life I could offer; have I done less?"

"Surely not, in providing. But a woman wants more of her man, honey. She wants to see him tall in his pride, grow in his pride. How do you reckon a woman feels when her man backs off from a bigmouth ninny like O'Brien who swears he can lick you seven ways to sundown? Man with gumption and spirit just doesn't abide that kind of public talk."

"Words," Lambeth said. "Good Lord, Lila Mae. I'm not a child to stand about with a chip on my shoulder, waiting for a bully to knock it off." He rose abruptly and went to pour another drink.

Lila Mae bit her lip, thinking bleakly, *This is not the way. But I have to find one—I have to,* while a small desperate panic crowded her thoughts. Memory, bitter as it was, was her ally to ambition; time was the enemy. She was no longer a girl; this was the chance for which she had planned and waited, her woman's weapons of face and body too swift-fading a part of her remaining life for her to afford a failure now.

42

"Reckon I'll take a breath of air," she sighed, and went to her room for a shawl. She went out the front way, but then skirted the house at a casual walk. The timbered ridge rose sharply behind it, and locating a crooked footpath that wound up through dark-aisled pines, she swiftly followed it. A mottling of dim moonlight picked out her way, and shortly she broke into an open glade.

"Boo," Charley Starr said idly, as she halted. Lila Mae peered against a bank of dark brush; it rustled and stirred as he stepped into the open, the coal of his cigarette vivid in the night. His next words were shaded by irritation: "Took you long enough."

"That so? I never jumped yet to your beck and call, Charley, not here or before. Just you remember it."

"So long as I never catch you jumping to another man's," Charley said hard and low, snapping his cigarette away. "Come here." His hands and lips were rough, and she stiffened against them, then placed her flat palms against his chest till he stepped back. His hooded eyes were ugly against moonlight, and his breathing was deep and hoarse with anger.

Lila Mae said with a peculiar flatness, "You could do with a bath, my friend. Your manners could stand some cleaning up too."

He half-lifted his hand and then lowered it, which touched her with cool amusement. He had struck her only once, a long time ago, and had not made that mistake again. A woman, Lila Mae had found, owned a strength that could win over any brute force, if she knew about it quite thoroughly.

Charley Starr said thickly, "Wetnursing cows is not dilettante's fare, my sweet, and I wouldn't be except at your behest."

"That's right," she said tartly, adjusting her shawl. "And soon's you start filling your boots for the reason you're here, you can expect better. I didn't expect to find Senor Velez enjoying good health, time I got back from Soledad."

Starr swore under his breath, stepping off a restless circle with his thumbs rammed in his belt. He told her about the business with the sheepherder two days ago; and of how again last night Brazos Kane had given him some bad moments. His voice held a harried baffled fury: "That redheaded runt has the Indian sign on me. I can feel it in my bones, by God."

"Don't be a fool," Lila Mae said curtly. "That doesn't sound like you, Charley. Letting a mere happening or so get under your hide. Not afraid of him, are you?"

"No." Charley Starr's gaze was slitted and brooding.

43

"Something else. Not sure what, maybe the name. Just the name alone. Kane."

"You're making no sense," she said impatiently. "No point getting fretful about it; look at things as they stand. Hazing that sheepherder was fair clumsy of you, honey. Seems you could set your sights higher than a poor greaser sheepman. We need something that will hit Montalvo where it hurts, a way of provoking O'Brien that'll put our side solidly in the right, to John's satisfaction."

"Damned small leeway for any sort of move," he muttered, "with that Velez breathing down my neck. He split up me, Pinto and Stu yesterday."

"What did you expect, now you've put him on his guard? No telling how much he suspects. Best thing you can do about Velez is let him alone, now you've botched your try. Just one move, Charley." Her voice softened, intimate and urgent at once. "One good solid move that'll provoke O'Brien; if he's provoked enough, he'll strike back, and then John will have to fight. He'll need a fighting force then, and a man who can head it. You."

"You must be slipping," Starr said dourly. "Drove the poor bastard to drink, and he won't come across for you."

Lila Mae's lip curled gently. "My Johnny's such a little gentleman, learned the code on the playing field of Rugby, all that rot. I can't urge him any more baldly without making him suspicious. John is mainly a fool where I'm concerned." Her voice hardened again. "That high summer grass is the heart of this basin, Charley. The outfit that controls it is the power here. Given time and growth, the whole power. Only way to push O'Brien off is fight him, and touching it off is just the start. It's got to be fought to a finish, and it's got to be won."

He watched her face, a strangeness in his regard. "You've come a long way since Albuquerque, Lila. A rich husband, big ranch. And you're not about to stop."

"Not for anything." It was time to reassure him; she let her face soften demurely. "Not till Lila has what she wants, and part of it's you, honey. . . . but you got to earn it." Her hands moved lightly to his shoulders. "One thing to be said about all this cownursin', it's filled you out real nice."

His hands tightened on her waist; she gave herself to the embrace fully, knowing his hunger of old, and in it her utter control over him. For a moment the brute magnetism of him swayed her, but a cold still voice told her that she wanted more, far more. Charley would have his place when the time came, but in her shadow; probably he knew as much, but Charley's life-wants had always been limited. She had discarded him once for that reason: since then she had made her own way and found it to her liking. Now he was a useful appendage, like a third hand, to her ends.

Contacting him several weeks back had presented no difficulty; Soledad was just below the Two Troughs county line, and Soledad—where Charley intermittently took up with a wild crowd of cardsharps, gunmen and unproven rustlers—had always been his favorite stamping grounds. A letter posted there would reach him sooner or later, and did.

"Seems to me," he murmured against her ear, "we've been overlooking the obvious. One bullet would make you a widow and solve both our problems."

She stirred her head in quick negation. "No. I don't want that."

Charley moved her gently off from him, a wicked note touching his faint lisp. "You wouldn't try to renege on me, would you, puss?"

"You know better than that. We're the same kind, you and I. I don't reckon to spend the rest of my life with a cricket field code in a tweed suit. I need a man who understands me, and you have no damnfool illusions concerning Lila Mae. That suits me fine. Johnny's time will come, don't you fret, but he's not in the same case as his greaser foreman. We could have put Velez down and set the blame so's not to point any fingers at us. Be a sight harder to do for Johnny boy without raising suspicion, him being my husband. I'm his sole heir, remember. Anything happens to him under suspicious circumstances, dear Mr. Keogh might start checking back. That sheriff doesn't see people, just law-abiders and law-breakers. If he learns we ran a gambling casino together in Albuquerque . . . got shut down by the law for shady dealing to boot . . ."

"All right, all right. What's the answer?"

"The answer's we go careful, to see no blame touches us. Say, if in a pitched fight between Montalvo and Nugget a bullet found him. Or if they caught him from ambush . . ."

"Sure," Charley Starr said softly. "But first you need a fight. How do you get it?"

"That's what you're here to find out," she said coldly. "You're on range daily, you and your two boys, and I'm not. Won't be easy now you're split up, but you'll have to keep watching for a way. Won't take much of an incident to nettle a hothead like O'Brien—but this time you make it

45

good." She paused reflectively. "This Kane fellow, Charley. He could be useful. You ought to mend fence a bit, cultivate the man . . ."

"The hell with that," Charley Starr said with a hating intensity. "I'd as soon bed with a sidewinder. His day's coming too, and I'll be around then."

Charley's cool and unruffled face rarely broke to his streak of dark temper, but Lila Mae had bested him often enough with her woman's weapons to know the signs. Charley's backbone was his raw pride, and this Brazos Kane had shaken it. At such times, she had learned, it was best to sweeten the starch.

"Surely, honey, anyhow you want it. Just an idea. But no trouble with him till this other is settled, promise? Or I might just cultivate him myself."

Half-mollified by the teasing note, he growled, "You likely would, too. You know how to blood a man where he lives, for sure."

"There's a cautery for that, and it won't hurt a bit. Here, honey. Right here . . ."

CHAPTER SIX

THE TOUGH ROUTINE of scouring half-wild steers out of the rugged north breaks went on for several days—a punishing grind that wore a man down till his mind picked sluggishly at even a deep concern. Brazos went over it again, squatting in the shade of a piñon with Simon Jack Pima. The two of them were taking a breather and a smoke after cleaning out a scrub oak thicket deep to the northwest.

A desperation had begun to thread Brazos' impatience. For three nights running he had lingered outside the bunkhouse after lights out, watching the main house. But Lambeth or his wife were accustomed to burning the late oil, and twice he'd quit his vigil and turned in, wary against arousing suspicion. His tardiness after lights out drew some complaints from the crew, but was put down to a personal quirk.

Last night he'd been in luck; the lights in the main house had soon followed the bunkhouse into darkness. The bedrooms, including the Mexican housemaid's, were located toward the front of the house, and without much concern that he might arouse their occupants, he'd promptly set to working open the window of the ranch office at the rear. For a half hour he had rifled gingerly through Lambeth's desk and the battered filing cabinet; not daring to light a lamp, he had burned innumerable matches, hand-cupped, studying account books, tally records, invoices, bills, and receipts. The bulk of the records, yellow with age, dated from the previous ownership, and the spare entries since were all in order and quite conventional. The books balanced, and there were notes to cover every entry. Brazos had covered the whole room thoroughly, chafing with futility. A man would keep any sentimental but dangerous links with his past in a secret place; to search Lambeth's room was a temptation out of the question while its tenant hung close to the house and his liquor source.

Brazos had carefully erased all traces of his search down to the last burned matchhead and returned to the bunkhouse, knowing in the bitter drowsiness before sleep came that he faced a quandary: wait and watch for some chance slip on Lambeth's part or force the issue at gunpoint. *But if he's a real tough nut, he won't scare by a bluff.* Wringing a confession from a man you were unsure of was an ugly prospect, even if he hadn't been saddled by a really deep uncertainty about Lambeth. *So where does that leave you?*

He dragged deeply on his cigarette, considering the bleak shape of matters. What did he really know about Pop's killer? That he was a professional gambler or posed as one, his physical appearance which could be partly changed, the slender connection of a general locale the man had mentioned to the bartender Seeley, and that he had a lot of money to spend but might have cached it away. If he was in the area at all and he was not Lambeth, then who? *And supposing you find him and the money too? What then?* He had the acrid realization that he hadn't been willing to face till now: that the prospect of developing his horse ranch had gone oddly tasteless since the way of life that centered it was gone. For good or bad, his life with Pop Melaven had been the only way he knew.

"Brazos fella damn little talk," Simon Jack Pima said, dousing his cigarette in the ground and then rising in a lithe motion. "Plenty work, no talk. Good."

"That why you side me?"

"Hunh."

They moved to their horses, and Brazos grinned, stepping into the saddle. The Nugget men, except for Charley Starr and his pair, had accepted him; he had a friend in Velez and a partner of sorts in the taciturn Pima.

"Yourself, you're a sight handier with horses than your mouth," Brazos observed, as they climbed their horses across a flinty ridge. "I make Simon Jack a mission name."

"Hunh. Run away mission when boy. Not like. Alla time talk, smooth preacher talk. Man life better. Hunt, wrangle horse, punch cow, catchem drunk. You-me catchem drunk mebbe sometime."

"Maybe."

Riding in comfortable silence then, they topped the ridge and descended its sudden drop in a rattle of granite scale. The canyon below was clean, except for a lonesome mulberry-colored steer who made a crashing retreat into upcanyon brush. The two men threaded the thickets and broke into the clear, finding the old steer boxed against a dead end. He was wicked-eyed at bay, whipping his tail; his hide was networked with ancient scars, and his horns looked sharp as needles.

48

"Hell, even his tallow would make stringy."

"Ramon say bring 'em all."

"Head him out. I'll take the right."

They broke apart, folding their ropes double, and skirted onto the steer from either side. Brazos gave a hoarse yell and spurred in, swinging his rope. The steer's nostrils flared and he spooked sidelong instead of ahead. Simon Jack reined off too late, and a slashing horntip drew blood on his pinto's chest; the animal reared and plunged as the steer went past, and Simon Jack lost his saddle as his horse bolted away.

The Pima hit the ground with a horsebreaker's aplomb, his body loose as a sack of meal. But rolling over twice, met a rough boulder with his head. He went limp in a stunned sprawl, as the steer, after making a panicky lunge at the flanking wall, wheeled and charged downcanyon. The Pima was in his path, and there was no time to head him aside. Brazos drew and fired by blurred instinct, placing two shots behind the forehock. The mulberry steer crashed to its knees and half-cartwheeled, kicking onto its side. It was still almost at once, and Brazos piled from his saddle and dropped down by Simon Jack.

The Pima grunted and stirred, and Brazos eased him to his feet. He rubbed his head, stoically eying the dead steer. "Good shoot. No much mouth, you plenty gun."

"Make it double till we find your horse?"

"Hunh." The Pima's eyes flickered. "Not forget." He clamped a sinewy hand over Brazos' shoulder. "Friend."

"I was handy. Let's get on out." With Simon Jack mounted behind, they started out of the canyon, breaking brush. As they came on the pinto grazing quietly in a pocket of grass, a shot sent a fusillade of echoes across the stony hills. It was followed by two more close together, and Brazos said tautly, "Get mounted. We better see about that."

The Pima grunted and slid to the ground, and whistled up the pinto. Brazos, not waiting, pushed his blue up over the ridge and angled toward the west. These breaks lay almost beneath the rim of the plateau where Montalvo high grass began, and the Montalvo vaqueros had been working them too. This had concerned Velez enough to prompt his direct order that the Nugget hands go out of their way to avoid trouble, and those sudden shots could mean anything

The spattering of gunfire continued as he came onto the summit of a long rise. Below, a bunchgrass flat studded by rock slabs rolled off to a sharp terminus at the bulging wall of the lower plateau. He saw a small jag of cattle milling confusedly, and through the hazy wind drift of dust, deep smudges of powdersmoke blossoming among the rocks. On this side, two men at widely separated points appeared to be exchanging fire with one or more holed up halfway on the flat.

Brazos came off the rise at a stretching run, knowing he could draw fire at any moment. A rifle slug screamed off a near rock, and he sank low in the saddle, speed his only ally on this open slope till it tapered off into the rocks and bunchgrass. There he dismounted and left his horse, and worked in afoot toward the nearest man's position. Simon Jack wasn't far behind, and as he reached the bottom of the rise, Brazos waved him on. He waited till the Pima, loping noiselessly over the rocks, dropped to his side among them.

An open belt of sand and bunchgrass lay ahead, and where it ended a man crouched behind an upended slab, anonymous in the wind-tattered dust. A roan horse stood by, leaning hipshot to windward; Simon Jack grunted. "Hunh. Starr horse." As he spoke, the second rifleman left cover twenty yards away, his angular body bent in an awkward crouch as he skirted toward the right.

"DeVries," Brazos said. "He's yours."

"We stop?"

"Before someone gets hurt. Velez and the others are scattered way north and east of here. Even if the shots bring 'em, it'd be too late."

Simon Jack grunted his assent; he loped away, fading into the dust and rocks like a dusky shadow. DeVries began to fire from a fresh position at the shallow barricade where the enemy, doubtless Montalvo men, had forted up. The advantage lay against them, caught on an open rockfree stretch except for their shelter, while the Nugget pair could maneuver freely in the surrounding rocks. Again DeVries was changing position, obviously working behind them while Charley Starr laid the covering fire.

A heavy furl of dust blew across the open ground. Before it eddied off, Brazos scrambled over the rocks and ran low and fast, his gun butt gritty against his sweating palm. Charley Starr heard him and started around on his haunches, and now Brazos pulled up, planting his heels apart. A good six yards still separated them, but Starr, caught in an awkward squat, froze that way.

"Go ahead," Brazos said. "Try it or throw it away, but go ahead."

Charley Starr spat; he squinted and licked dust from his

lips and said, "You bastard," as he tossed his rifle into the open. He raised his hands shifting to his feet, and Brazos, moving forward, favored him with a hard grin. "The hogleg, Charley."

Hot-eyed, Starr lifted his sidearm and threw it down. "It's the last time for you, drifter. Laugh it up. You won't cross me again."

"You have a bad eye today, Charley. Got your story all ready?"

Starr said nothing. Brazos, grinning, motioned toward the upended rock slab. "Get up there."

"You bastard."

"That's two of us, but you'll be the dead one if you can't stop it."

Starr tugged his hat aslant against the blowing dust, turned and climbed the slab till his head and shoulders topped it. "All the way," Brazos told him. "Get up there."

"By God, you want to get me killed!"

"Your choice." Brazos thumbed his hammer to full cock, and Charley Starr swore viciously and clambered fully atop the abutment; he waved his hands shouting hoarsely. The Montalvo men held their fire, waiting, and Brazos said, "You have the devil's luck, Charley. I'd blow you off that rock myself. Tell them we'll meet them halfway."

"You're crazy!"

"Only if it was them started it, and we know different, don't we? Tell them."

Starr cupped his hands to his mouth and shouted again. Then, as Brazos felt a first sharp concern for Simon Jack, the Pima tramped into sight with Pinto DeVries in tow. And Brazos remembered only now that Simon Jack carried no gun. DeVries was being prodded ahead of the slim Indian, the keen goad of a knifetip nudging his short ribs. Wordlessly the Pima handed him DeVries' pistol, and Brazos tossed it over by Starr's and motioned with his gun. "All right, let's get out there."

They moved into the open, and the two vaqueros left cover now and came warily to meet them, their guns at the ready. One was hardly more than a boy, his soft beardless face working with a choking rage. The left arm of his *charro* jacket was soaked with blood, tourniqueted crudely above the elbow by a twisted bandanna and a stick. The other Mexican was middle-aged, his square and rugged face darkly expressionless; only his eyes smoldered with his thoughts as he drew up facing them.

51

"So you fight among yourselves," he said in good English frosted by contempt. "So like the Anglos. You cannot agree even on how best to make trouble for greasers."

"No more trouble unless you want it," Brazos said. "How did this start?"

"We were combing out the strays, like you. Much stock drifts into these breaks in the winter—ours and yours. These men came up and said we were rustling."

Charley Starr said softly, "There are a half-dozen Nugget brands in that bunch, and they were pushing them toward Montalvo."

"Yes," the Mexican said coldly. "We came on this mixed bunch, most of them, in a canyon pocket deep in the brush. It was easiest to push them out all at once, down to this flat which happens to lay toward Montalvo. Here we would have cut them and pushed our own on west. Before we started, these two rode down on us. I tried to talk, but they were of no mind to hear it."

"Now," Charley Starr said, "I'll hear out a white man—"

"Shut up," Brazos said gently, and looked back at the older Mexican. "Mind saying your name?"

"Armando Pesquiera. This young one is Jaime Elias."

"Brazos Kane. If there's more, better tell it now."

Pesquiera studied Brazos a long moment, stroking a calloused thumb along the breech of his down-slanted rifle. "We denied what they said, and the fat one called us liars—and other things. Jaime is young, his blood is quick. As a man will, called such things, he took it badly; then this big one, the fair man, shot him."

"Only when he pulled on Stu," put in Charley Starr. "That right?"

"Yes," Pesquiera turned the word off his tongue with a soft contempt. "Only then. And so we broke for the rocks, and there was a lot of shooting."

"You asked for that."

"Yes," Pesquiera smiled icily. "Of a certainty."

The advantage that Starr had seized here, Brazos reflected, was calculated beyond simply twisting an innocent situation to his use. If he later told only the bald-faced truth of what had happened, the ugly understrata of an Anglo's telling against a Mexican's would bear in his favor.

"Serious charge, that. Cattle-stealing. It's got men hung."

Pesquiera's eyes were edged like obsidian, asking nothing, expecting nothing. "It is very serious—Anglo."

"Could lead to a lot worse, in this case." Brazos slanted a sultry stare at Starr's bland face. "Things as they are, it could get a whole lot of men killed."

"This," Pesquiera murmured, "could happen."

"Other hand, Charley here could have made a mistake." A faint, crooked smile touched Starr's lips, and Brazos thought then, *The son of a bitch won't let go of it; he knows he's on safe ground, win or lose. No mistake, but it could have been.* "Charley," he said quietly, "I ought to shoot you now."

"Well," Charley Starr grinned, "that's up to you, naturally."

Brazos, grinning too, said, "I'm like you, Charley. I can wait." And to Pesquiera: "I'd let this go by with no mention to your boss. It's a lot to ask."

Pesquiera hesitated, then nodded his understanding. "Maybe that is best." His eyes hardened on Starr and DeVries. "But these two, do they get by with this?"

"Just a minute." He had spotted a half-dozen riders moving up from the southeast, coming fast in a tight bunch. *Montalvo,* he thought, and bringing his gaze to the north ridges, saw the three horsemen sloping off this way. *Nugget.* In the next few minutes it could break wide open, and any effort to stop it could not be one-sided. He brought his eyes back to Pesquiera. "Will you let me handle it?"

"No!" Jaime Elias said hotly. "No, Armando." The fierce unthinking gesture of his hurt arm brought a quick wince. "This one, he's just another Anglo."

"Be patient, Jaime. You are lucky that you were only born when God made you a fool; you may grow out of it in time." The boy flushed and lowered his sullen eyes. Pesquiera gave Brazos another raking and merciless study, and nodded. "Yes, I will trust you—to see that justice is done?"

"I meant that," Brazos agreed. He returned his attention to the coming Nugget men, seeing with relief that the lead rider was Velez. The others were Mose Cruikshank and towheaded Link Bardine—both steady heads. Both groups of riders slowed now, and coming at a cautious trot, reached the central flat at the same time. Brazos saw the grim-faced vaqueros were ranked respectfully behind a young woman, and remembered a mention of O'Brien's daughter. She sat her sidesaddle with a horsewoman's relaxed poise that easily accommodated her mettlesome black's prancing, bringing him under control on a gentle rein. "Ramon—buenas dias."

Velez touched his hat with dry courtesy, nodding toward the vaqueros. "These have a new foreman, Raquel?"

"I was riding by the river forking and heard the shots," she said calmly. "Then I met the men—and that is bad irony, Ramon."

"Maybe. I am not a man of words. Now, Brazos, what is this about?"

Brazos told it with brevity, shuttling his gaze from face to face, knowing the immediate danger was past, the truce sealed by a woman's presence. Velez stroked his gray mustache with a finger; he said pointedly, "You think Armando and Jaime have the right of it?"

"I do," Brazos said flatly. "I'd tell it to Mr. Lambeth that way. Will you back me?"

"Why not?" DeVries murmured. "Chilipickers are like burrs. They just naturally hang together."

"Shut your mouth, Pinto." Charley Starr's tone was even and pleasant. "Ramon's been waiting on a solid excuse to fire us, is all. Think you have it, Ramon?"

Velez said curtly, "We'll see," glancing at the girl. "Does this satisfy you?"

A small frown puckered her brow. "If there was a wrong done here, it was to Armando and Jaime. They are not thieves."

Velez looked at them questioningly, and Pesquiera said: "Do I speak for you, Jaime?" Elias, after a scowling pause, gave his reluctant nod. "Then," said Pesquiera, his proud face impassive, "we are satisfied," and cleared his throat gently. "One thing, senorita. I think the mayordomo, your father, should not hear of this, though you speak for him."

"Nobody speaks for Mike O'Brien." She smiled a little. "You know that as well as I, Armando."

"Truly, senorita. That is why I say this." Pesquiera's words softened with stubborn insistence, and Brazos knew he was fortunate in his ally. A good man strong in his loyalty, but ready to court displeasure of the mayordomo's daughter to stand by his point—aware of his mayordomo's well-known temper.

"And I agree, Armando. Anyway I left it up to you." She gave Velez a friendly nod. "It's been a long time, Ramon. Will you say hello for me, to Delores?"

"That, surely."

She looked at Brazos then, and he thought that her eyes did not flatter a man; they were clearest gray, full of a merciless and searching candor, like a child's. She was a slight but not frail girl, with a boyish and slim-muscled grace about her. Her face was thin and finely angled, and she wore

54

her dark brown hair carelessly clubbed at the back of her head. Her faded yellow waist and brown merino riding skirt and scuffed boots had a look of well-worn comfort.

"This man, I think, stopped it?" Pesquiera gave an assenting nod, and she said: "I would like to speak to him, Ramon."

"Surely. Go with God, Raquel."

"Go with God, Ramon."

"Join us at the headquarters then," Velez told Brazos, and turned his cold regard on Sholto and Charley Starr. "Now we'll get your horses."

The Nugget men swung away and moved off, and Pesquiera said quietly to Brazos, "It's done, senor. My thanks."

"No," Brazos said. "Mine."

Pesquiera's mouth quirked; he nodded, and went to get his and Elias' horses. Raquel let the cool gravity of her gaze touch the vaqueros, man by man. "There must be no word of this to my father—Jaime was shot by accident. You all understand this?"

There were murmurs and nods of assent, and then she said kindly, "Jaime, ride home quickly. I will be there soon to tend your arm."

Elias' face was sullen. He took his reins as Pesquiera led his horse up, stonily refusing assistance as he mounted. The vaqueros began to cut the bunched cattle, hoorawing their own away west. Raquel impatiently shook her head as Brazos made a move to help her dismount; her skirt hung up briefly as she stepped down and she freed it with a tug and came around to face him, her warm olive skin faintly flushed. "I'm Raquel O'Brien—Brazos?"

"Kane."

"It was Armando's place to say, but I will too. I'm sure we have you to thank for stopping something worse."

"I was handy."

"Not only that." The bay nuzzled her shoulder, and she stroked its nose, her wide mouth tucked at the corners by an absent smile. "We're all very close, you see, at Montalvo. Not the same as when my mother's family ruled the basin in their aloof, lordly way. The peons were peons, kept aware of their station. My father has given them more, a touch of Anglo democracy, a pride in themselves as people. He works and plays at their side; he loves their way of life and lets them know it, and they worship him for it." She paused, with a self-conscious smile. "I guess all I'm trying to say is that we at Montalvo are really one in our feeling—to help one of us makes you the friend of all." She seemed to fumble, and he sensed that social talk came as awkwardly to her as it did to him. "Brazos—that is a strange name. Isn't that a river?"

"Yes, ma'am, in Texas. My father settled by it, and I was named after it."

"Oh." She kneaded her lip between her teeth, scowled at her quirt, and slapped it against her dusty skirt. Then gave him a sudden look. "I think . . . now I remember, you helped Pepe Garcia. I was visiting with Pilar, Armando Pesquiera's wife, and she said Juana told her—Juana is their daughter and Pepe's wife. But . . ." She smiled slowly. "Perhaps you were only handy."

Brazos grinned. Her glance moved past him, and he looked over his shoulder. The blue had trotted into sight, and he whickered softly as he came up, nudging Brazos' arm. Brazos cuffed him away with a rough fondness, and saw that Raquel's eyes were alive with interest. "Caught him, raised him from a colt," he explained. "I'm a horse trapper."

"How wonderful!"

He looked at her with an odd disbelief, and saw then that she meant it. He said as a matter of courtesy, "Yours is a fine animal, ma'am. Arabian?"

"He's descended from stock my ancestors brought from Spain." Her talk came with a quick animation then, and knowing that feeling for good horses, Brazos warmed to the subject and talked at length of his knowledge and experience—a thing always taken for granted. She was an unaffected girl, he thought, watching her face change moods, and had been a tomboyish gamin for sure. He wondered about that, remembering his meeting with Mike O'Brien. A bluff rough open-faced man who probably gave his motherless girl a fairly free rein. *But he wouldn't fancy this a damn bit,* Brazos thought, and felt a shade uneasy on his own hook; he had no damned business even talking to a girl like this one.

She broke off in the middle of a sentence, with an embarrassed laugh. "Oh, good heavens. I forgot about Jaime's arm. I must be getting home—and you have other business, Mr. Kane. I wish . . . we might talk again."

He said nothing to that, and this time she waited for his assistance as she mounted, afterward looking at him gravely. "I hope that Mr. Lambeth will discharge those two men."

Brazos shook his head. "Wish I could answer for him—but I can't."

"I understand." Her smile was full and friendly, but a

56

trace of shyness lingered in her words. "I can't give you the welcome of our house. Unless . . . if you ever leave Nugget . . ."

"Thank you." He touched his hat. "I don't look forward to that very soon, ma'am."

CHAPTER SEVEN

JOHN LAMBETH paced a slow circle around the parlor, listening to Velez' quiet words. Lila Mae listened composedly, hands clasped on her knees. Instinct warned her that this was a time to be demure and silent as a good wife should be, but the sting of cold anger was held tightly in her. Charley had played the hand she had dealt him well enough, but he'd been a careless fool in the doing. *If John wants to fire him, you'll have a time convincing him otherwise.*

As Velez ceased talking, John halted a foot from Charley, saying sharply, "Do you have anything to say to that?"

Charley Starr stood with his hat in hands, his eyes lowered in a dutiful but stubborn way. "Only what I've said, sir. The simple truth."

"But suppose you were wrong, man! Did you consider the consequences?"

Charley Starr drew a long breath and let it out, lifting his eyes. Lila Mae conceded him credit for one thing; Charley, an excellent gambler, could play a part to the hilt. "Mr. Lambeth, this is a hard country. There is an answer to cattle thieves, and Pinto and I were about to give it when Kane and the Indian stepped in. Sir, there is another side to the coin; turn it over. I believe that you hired Stu, Pinto and myself to head off trouble?"

"But not make it, Starr."

"Mr. Lambeth," Charley said with a persuasive softness, "you don't understand this country or the kind of man it produces. Here, let a man take an inch and he'll seize a yard. Let him take advantage of you once, only once, and get away with it, and he'll make bold to carry the trouble you want to head off directly to your doorstep."

Lambeth hesitated, frowning. "This is assuming—"

"Yes, sir," Charley Starr said flatly. "I named those men thieves; I still think they are, and I think we did right. *We* didn't start the gunplay, remember." He let his voice sink in a confiding, pointed way. "I have to say this, Mr. Lambeth. I'm a schooled man like yourself, and I despise bigotry. But—

the plain fact is, these Mexicans are born inevitable and hopeless thieves. The Indian in them, of course—you know how Indians are—seize every damned thing that isn't nailed down. I know you're a man who listens to experience, and those are the hard facts. Ramon is different, of course, but he's lived among white men—"

"Senor," Velez broke in with a cold and controlled fury, "I had sent these two to work well apart and with others. Let them tell how they happened together on the Montalvo men."

"Is that true, Starr?" Lambeth said it almost abstractedly, gnawing his lip as if mulling over Charley's speech.

"Pinto and Stu and I are used to working together." There was a hint of bland mockery in the look Charley sent Velez, Brazos Kane and Simon Jack Pima, who stood together by the door. DeVries stood apart, his stance one of hipshot indifference. "Pinto and I had finished our assigned chores, then happened across each other and were working south when we found the Mexicans. And acted accordingly. The foreman didn't happen to give any direct orders to the contrary. If he didn't want us siding each other, he might have said so."

"Yes," Velez breathed, "that was a mistake."

"Come, come," Lambeth said irritably. "Fair play, Ramon, eh?"

Lila Mae felt a strong wash of relief now, and curbed an urge to laugh aloud. Charley had sowed a seed of doubt in John's Anglo-Saxon soul, while at the same time John's stubborn conviction of his own fairmindedness was playing, for once, into her hands. She was aware then of the hard, watchful stare of Brazos Kane and demurely lowered her eyes, irritably wondering whether he suspected something. Probably he was only remembering her own sentiments about greasers, but she thought coldly, *Damn the fellow's insolence. He's the one. Charley was right; he has to be dealt with somehow.*

"Starr, I don't know whether you were right or wrong. But from now on, whatever you suspect, I'll decide on the measures to be taken. Kindly consult me before you leap."

"Yes, sir," Charley murmured.

"Senor," Velez said harshly, "the decision is yours, but let me remark—"

"I understand," Lambeth said curtly. "Starr, whatever your personal feelings, you and Devries and Sholto will obey Ramon's orders implicitly. Is that clear?"

"Yes, sir," Charley said dutifully. "Will that be all?"

"You and DeVries have put in a busy morning. Suppose you knock off the day and think over what I said."

John understood men's ways as well as he understood women's badly, Lila Mae reflected. Allowing matters between Charley and Velez to boil back to a simmer by keeping them apart awhile, would give her an immediate chance to see Charley alone. When the men had left the room, she rose and walked to John as he stood looking out the window, hands clasped at his back.

"Honey, you handled that just right. I'm proud of you."

"I wonder." Lambeth swung toward her, gnawing his lip. "What did you think of Starr's little speech?"

"Why, I'm sure he's perfectly sincere. It's sure enough as he says; this is a rough country. . . ."

"Yes, that's the point." Lambeth's eyes were bleakly musing. "One I may have given too little attention. Have I been wrong? Does O'Brien think he can push me as far as he likes and get away with it?"

At last, ran Lila Mae's exultant thought. "Well, honey, if you'll mind, that's what I've been saying all along." And at his soft chuckle: "Did I say something funny?"

"I'm sorry, my dear." He patted her arm tolerantly. "But after all, what does a gently-bred young woman know about such things? Let the men handle men's affairs, eh?"

And this time she did laugh, with a wry self-deprecation. All along she had tried to wear him down with persuasive vehemence, forgetting that for such a man a woman was no person but a stainless angel sweetly marbled on a pedestal; for her to step from it was only, to him, disturbing unreality. Charley he at least respected as a world-wise tough who knew his business, and so gave weight to his opinions.

"Declare," she murmured. "I *am* a little goose."

"Not at all," he said gallantly. "Matter of fact you may have chanced on the truth. Understand, I'm only saying that Starr *may* have hit the nail squarely." He gave a slow absent nod. "We'll go along as we've been, but bearing it in mind."

It was an opening wedge, and Lila Mae did not overplay her hand. *Now you know, go carefully; give him his pride.* She murmured a quiet agreement and excused herself, going directly to her room and leaving him with his thoughts.

Shortly after the noon meal, she left the house and strolled up the piney ridge back of the house. She seated herself on the needle-carpeted slope where, through the screening trees, she had a good view of the ranchlot. She saw Ramon Velez' Delores leave their small house and scatter feed to her flock of chickens. She studied Velez' wife through narrowed lids, sensitive to the woman's antagonism but wasting no thought on it. Lila Mae had a man's mind unvictimized by a man's instincts, and her dislike for her own sex was contemptuous and thorough.

When, presently, Charley and Pinto DeVries left the cook-shack and headed for the stable, she rose, dusted pine needles from her skirt, and sauntered idly down off the slope. She was aware of Delores Velez' sharp eyes following her, and moved on past the carriage shed. When it cut her off securely, she hurried up back of the stable and slipped through the rear door into its runway.

Her nostrils twitched at the smell of dank manure, heavy and suffocating. The two men were talking quietly by a window, and glancing her way, Charley said, "All right, Pinto, later." DeVries nodded, and slouched out the front way. As she came over to Starr, he settled his back to the log wall, arms folded, watching her stonily.

"Well," she said acridly. "You pretty close to made an unholy botch of things, didn't you?"

Charley fumbled a cigar from his pocket, bit off the end and spat it out. "That Kane. I mean to settle with him, Lila, and not a month from now. Bastard's like a black cat."

"Indian sign, rot!" she said with a flat vehemence that arrested the cigar short of his lips. "He and the Injun were working nearer than you thought, that's all! Get a hold on yourself!"

"No. It was ripe and ready, we even got the Mexes to pull the first gun, and there he was. Something else, though." He ground the cigar between his teeth. "Told you that name meant something—Kane. Now it comes to me."

Lila Mae's eyes pinched gently at the corners. "Been a long time since Albuquerque, and just maybe there's a thing or so you haven't told me. Wouldn't be that you're wanted for something, Charley?"

"Suppose I was?"

"And suppose this Kane's a lawman?"

"Nothing like that." He took the cigar from his mouth, not looking at her, and shredded it slowly in his fist. "I robbed a man of a good piece of money. It comes back that he mentioned his partner's name while drunk. Kane, and he's a horse trapper, I heard one of the crew say."

"Is that all, Charley? You wouldn't have done his partner real harm? Maybe killed him?"

"If I did?"

"You fool! Why didn't you say so? You think I want any truck with—" She bit her lip stifling a cry as his hands clamped with brittle force around her arms.

"Don't say it," he said with a low savagery. "Remember what you told me once? No future with Charley Starr; he was too slack and lowdown to ever make good. That was when I went on the drift, looking for the main chance. This was it: a drunk old mustanger with twelve thousand dollars in his poke. A good-sized stake I could invest in something big. Think I don't know what that makes me? What you made me? Only difference between Lambeth and me, I know you, my sweet. I know you." He let go of her then, breathing hard. "What sticks in your craw is this could foul up your stake here; not that Lambeth or me or ten more men could get killed filling your needs. So don't, by God, start getting selective about my sins."

She swung away, rubbing her arms and said bitterly, "You could have told me before."

"Hell, I looked for you up and down. You'd dropped out of sight. Then I got your letter; you needed only my help, not me. Not with a big ranch, a wealthy new husband, on your string. What could a man say to that? So I hid the money and came." He turned her by the shoulders. "It's still waiting for us, Lila—twelve thousand dollars. Doesn't why I did it mean a thing?"

Calmly she pulled away from his hands. "Tail between your legs and ready to run, is that it, Charley? And you want me to run with you. Well, it's just no dice, honey. I come higher than a few thousand now, a whole lot higher." His mouth twisted for words; she raised her hand sharply. "Just you brace up now, mister! Duck out if you want, but you'll go it alone. Stay on, and you'll go straight to the end of the line with Lila. Now, which?"

Charley Starr groaned under his breath; he hammered his fist against the sill of the high musty window. "All right—all right."

"Now that's settled, there's Kane. How much does he know?"

"Enough to track me here, for sure. Not enough to make his move yet, or he could have this morning. He had the chance." He stared at her wrathfully. "I told you he had to be settled. Now, by God!"

"Yes," she nodded curtly. "Thanks to you, he could pull the

roof down on us. I need you alive. Only it will go my way. I've had sufficient of your clumsy doing, my friend."

She stared with blank speculation at the fly-blown window, the idea nudging almost casually against her thoughts, and she probed it warily around. Of course—the stone that killed two birds. "Charley, I reckon I could just be a widow by this time tomorrow. How's that strike you?"

"Not too plain," he said narrowly. "You said it. Lose yourself a husband now and it'll draw fire on the two of us."

"Why honey, it surely won't, if it's known someone else did the job."

CHAPTER EIGHT

THE BRUSHPOPPING was nearly finished by this late afternoon, the crew flung out wide to clean out the last handful of scrubs. Brazos and Simon Jack broke apart to clean out a maze of coulees, and after hoorawing out a gaunt pair of strays, Brazos found himself alone. He sat his saddle and built a smoke over some solitary and irritable reflection.

After what had occurred this morning, he could no longer deny that he was getting deeply enmeshed in business that he considered none of his. He wasn't sure why, unless it was that his lonewolf inclinations had been shaped by a way of life that had died with Pop Melaven. A man's nature warmed to immediate concerns, and these were crowding him in a fresh direction. He could accept that; what made him uneasy was his dimming suspicion of John Lambeth. He was about convinced of the man's basic decency, and even the shred of doubt that remained no longer carried much force. *You're dead, Pop, and I can't change that.*

The thought had a ring of betrayal, and the habit of old feelings nudged him with a twinge of guilt. He dragged deeply on his cigarette, his eyes bleak. He owed Pop's memory more than that, and he couldn't discard an unpaid debt like an outworn boot; Pop was the only person he'd ever rightly owed a thing.

All right, he thought savagely, *all right!* Abruptly he pinched out his cigarette and dropped it, and swung the blue back toward the breaks. And then reined in, seeing a single rider emerge from the sloping timber east above the flats. He identified Lila Mae Lambeth's pale green riding costume, and thought, *now what the hell?* Earlier he had spotted her watching the work from a good distance, and feeling a nettling curiosity now, he settled back to wait till she rode up to him.

She made a pert and pretty sight in her smart riding outfit and nonsensical tilted hat with its wisp of veil. Her ride had stung her face with fresh color, and he was not deceived by the warmth of her smile. " 'Lo, there. I've been looking to talk to you."

"Yes'm."

"Alone." She ranged up by his stirrup, and a guarded un-ease touched him; what was she up to? "Don't be stand-offish, mister. Could be something in it for you."

Smilingly she twirled the horsehair quirt thonged to her wrist, and he said flatly, "What?"

Still smiling, she murmured, "This," and slashed the quirt across his neck. He flung his hand up by instinct, but she didn't strike again; she wheeled her horse around with a low brittle laugh, spurring the animal away with the same vicious deliberation that had marked the blow.

Brazos watched her go, rubbing the raw weal on his throat with a sense of baffled and formless anger. He could make nothing at all of this, and his anger dissolved in total bafflement as he rode back to pick up Simon Jack.

He met the Pima hazing a couple of scrubs onto the edge of the flat, and since it was about quitting time, the two of them rode to find Velez and the others. The crew made a dusty, dog-weary and irritable bunch as they rode back to headquarters. Since this morning, Velez' mood had been sharp with temper, reflected in his curt rough-driving of his men.

They wouldn't blame Velez if they had seen him, a man of pride who knew his job and did it well, get his nose rubbed in the dirt. Lambeth had made a show of arbitrating the situation fairly and of reprimanding Starr, but he'd committed the cardinal sin of not standing unequivocally behind his crew boss. Besides letting Starr's assertion that Velez' people were so many scavenging thieves pass without comment, he'd come within an ace of scolding his foreman like an erring little boy, and this Velez would not soon forgive or forget.

Stu Sholto, riding ahead of Brazos, was slumped with ex-haustion, his clothes brush-tattered and fouled with sweat and dirt—even more than usual. Brazos grinned, knowing that Velez, in taking out his wrath against Starr's and Pinto's chunky friend, had kept relentlessly after Stu's fat tail all afternoon, barking orders and insults and giving him the meanest stretches to brushpop. Brazos thought amusedly, *If he had all the lard he's shed today he'd have enough to butter his blisters.*

They came around the tack barn into the ranchyard, and swung past the bunkhouse, where Charley Starr was slacked on the washbench, boots crossed and hat tilted over his eyes. There was no sign of DeVries about. Idly, Starr nudged back his hat and squinted at Brazos as he passed, a faint grin tucking his wide mouth. Brazos was aware of his shirt chafing the raw whipmark on that side, and he thought narrowly, *like he knew*, and then dismissed the notion.

"Kane, I want to talk to you."

The sharp hail pulled his glance to the house veranda, where John Lambeth was standing in his shirt sleeves. He twitched the blue's head aside and split off from the crew, as they rode on to the corrals. He felt an uneasy caution as he reached the veranda. Lambeth, he saw, was wearing a holstered gun, and he had not gone armed before. His face had a pale, oddly pinched look, though his voice was crisply even:

"Get down. Come inside."

He turned, going into the house, and Brazos dismounted, left the blue at the rail, and followed. The light was fading, and the parlor held a cool gloom as he stepped inside.

Lila Mae Lambeth was pacing agitatedly back and forth, kneading a damp handkerchief in her hands. She still wore her riding costume, but now there was a rough tear in the shoulder, the sleeve torn half from its seam as if with force. Before Brazos had time to digest this, Lambeth turned, at the same time awkwardly yanking his gun from its holster. "As you are, Kane."

Brazos said slowly, "What is this?"

Not replying, Lambeth held the gun almost against his chest while he lifted Brazos' gun from its holster, rammed it into his own holster and stepped back. He said jerkily, "Tell it now, Lila Mae. As you told it to me."

She had halted, fearfully watching this byplay, and she pressed her kerchief to her lips with a choked little sound. "Oh, honey, I can't bear to. Not again! Can't you just—"

"I want this beggar to hear it. Then hear what he has to say."

With broken pauses and considerable tears she told of Brazos accosting her during her ride this afternoon and making a rough proposal, and then laying his hands on her. "He tore my habit . . . and I cut him hard . . . and ran my horse away and that's all there was," she sobbed. "Really, that's all."

Lambeth nodded gently. "Well, Kane, what have you to say?"

"I'd say," Brazos said tonelessly, "she's talking about twenty other men."

"Be careful, Kane." Lambeth's voice shook through its quiet

66

control. "Even a swine like you has a right to be heard, but be very damned careful of your words." He motioned slightly with his gun. "And while you're about it, remember the evidence on your own person speaks for itself."

Brazos passed his palm carefully over his neck, feeling the scour of a slow-lifting wrath as he weighed the thing in ugly clarity. It was a neat and damning frame—even without the confirming quirtwelt—but the baffling why of it held him mute, understanding that there was more than shallow spite behind this woman's actions. Though at this shaken moment, he could dredge up only a stunned blank.

"I'm waiting, Kane. Anything else?"

"Nothing," Brazos said softly, "that you'd listen to."

Lambeth nodded woodenly. "Very well. You'll leave the room, please, Lila Mae."

She raised a hand to her tear-stained cheek, a high false concern in her voice. "Honey—what're you going to do?"

Lambeth drew an unsteady breath and let it out. "Please." She sniffled once and turned, walking quickly from the room. Lambeth, not taking his eyes off Brazos, sidled across the room to an oaken cabinet and fumbled it open with his free hand. Brazos was unmoving, his feet set stubbornly apart. He was not a man to waste talk; this was as serious a bind as he'd ever known, but no use to argue with a love-blinded fool. With jerky and mechanical movements, Lambeth took an oblong wooden box from the cabinet. He set it on a table, but did not open it.

"Dueling pistols," he said quietly. "Precision weapons, hand-crafted and silver-mounted. Paired beauties if you go in for that sort of thing. Never did, myself. Always thought it was bloody nonsense. Heirlooms, though."

Brazos stared at him unbelievingly, thinking, *Why the poor green pup. He could shoot me on the spot, and no man would blame him.* Dueling pistols! The quiet idiocy of the notion was nearly laughable. And then his gaze sharpened, seeing the whiteness around Lambeth's mouth. *Hell, the idea's got him sick. Likely he's never held a handgun in his life, and now he's bound to kill a man with one.*

"Maybe," Brazos said softly, "I better talk after all. And you'd better listen."

Lambeth shook his head quickly. "No. Too late for that." He gave Brazos an odd, squinting regard. "You're a hard-looking customer, Kane, but somehow I wouldn't have thought this of you." He shrugged. "Well—bloody mess any way you go about it, but—honor, you know—a chap doesn't have a real choice."

Brazos slowly shook his head. "Mister, you're seven kinds of a fool."

"Quite. Could pull the trigger now and everyone would understand." Lambeth's voice held its crisp precision, but his face was nearly bloodless. "Unluckily, the bloody rotten code has it otherwise." He rapped the box with his knuckles. "Silly things, eh? Did a bit of target shooting with a Colt as a boy. Weapon's more to my taste, and I'm sure to yours. Doubt that a ratpoor mustanger to whom shells are surely dear will make too brilliant a show. A fair shake, I should say, and we'll make sure of keeping it private." He gestured at a rear hallway. "Now then."

"No."

"Damn you, yes." Lambeth thumbed back the hammer, and watching his eyes, Brazos knew he had the insides to carry it through here and now. He accepted the choice with a gray fatalism, knowing that all odds even, he could easily kill John Lambeth.

Then, swinging around to walk ahead of Lambeth, his eyes passed over an open window; he caught a stir of bushes beyond it that yanked his eyes back. Someone had been watching and listening there, and he knew it was not Lila Mae, who had gone to her room.

In deepening bewilderment, he said no more, but started through the house, Lambeth in step behind him. "We'll get off a bit from the place, and nobody will see us leave by the back. Once we're outside, you may think to run or shout for help. Either way I'll shoot at once. Clear?"

Brazos jerked his head in affirmation, and they went out through the kitchen. The slow timbered rise began a few yards from the back door, and Lambeth said with a dogged dispassion, "Straight ahead now." He started the long climb of the steepening slope, feeling the cool crawl of sweat between his shoulder blades. His nerves ached with the bite of helpless tension, and the empty irony of it washed through him. He had thought he might have come to kill this man, and now, utterly against his will, might be forced to.

Lambeth's steps were close at his back, and he heard his breath come thin and whistling. The flat slant of dying sunlight stretched long shadows upgrade, and softly gilded the gray pinebark and lay brown-gold on the litter of needleshed between the barred shadows. The quiet smell of death a man felt was only, Brazos knew, the last mood of day, the silence before twilight.

"Here," Lambeth said.

They had come to a shelf of flat ground that broke the lower swell of the vast ridge, and here the trees gave way to an open clearing, deeply oval in shape. The tight dark pines hemmed it all around, lending a somber loneliness to the place. Below, the clamor of the cook's triangle calling the crew to supper had a muted distance.

"Good enough for you?"

"No. Listen."

"For a woman-molester, you're a picky fellow. Over there, Kane." He took the gun from his holster and returned it to Brazos' own, and swung his gun in a level arc. Brazos let out his breath and tramped to one end of the clearing. When he turned there, Lambeth had backed off yards more.

A flicker of movement, half-sensed, barely touched the edge of Brazos' vision. Without turning his head he knew they had been followed here, and from the tail of his eye now he saw the sudden flow of sunlight and shadow across a man's form as he catfooted from the shelter of one giant pine to the next. *In his sock feet, whoever he is.* Then the man was out of sight, hugging a pinebole, but close to the clearing. Brazos had taken his glimpse of the intruder against the sun, but he thought, *Pinto DeVries for sure.*

Momentarily his thoughts braced against a cold blank, trying to weigh in this fresh and sudden fact. If Lila Mae Lambeth had set this up, being shrewd enough to know her husband stood small odds, she must have sent DeVries to cover him. And this much of the why flooded him with cold conviction: *She wants you dead.*

"I will count three." Lambeth said it with a cool precision, but his face had a fine glaze of sweat, his eyes strangely glazed too, like a man playing out a bad dream. Watching Brazos, he felt clumsily for his holster and slipped the gun into it.

"One."

Resigned to it then, Brazos stood as he was, hipshot and with his arms loose and slack. It had gone past words, and there was an obvious advantage open to him and no time to scruple against it. He waited for "Two" and then moved his hand, letting it blur down and up, and shot by instinct as the muzzle came level. Lambeth grunted; he caught his arm, his jaw sagging with a dumb shock. Brazos spun on his heel in the same instant that Pinto DeVries stepped partly to view in the fringing trees.

And he had his own moment of shock as DeVries' gun, arcing up, lined on John Lambeth's back. There was barely time to register the fact and tilt his own gun to bear. He shot DeVries in the chest and broke his aim, and the force of it smashed the thin gunman over backward like a rag-limp doll. It was a convulsive last reflex that sent the shot intended for John Lambeth angling wide above the rancher's head.

"You murdering devil," Lambeth hissed. He had sunk to his knees in his pain holding his arm, and he groped blindly with his left hand for the holstered gun. His face twisted whitely as his splayed fingers found the butt and closed, tugging the heavy Colt free.

He won't listen. The thought flashed and went, and Brazos broke in a crouching run for the downslope. As he reached the first trees, Lambeth's gun bellowed.

A smashing blow wrenched at his thigh in full run, and his leg gave way as he hit the slope. Helpless momentum sent him downward, a hand flung out to break his fall. He lit with a grunt on his face and belly, and his skidding plunge carried him two yards further on the slippery needle loam. He came to a stop with the outthrust heel of his palm furrowing the loam and his muscles relaxed in a stunned and momentary numbness before the full, tearing agony hit his thigh.

CHAPTER NINE

FOR A MOMENT, unmoving in his shocked pain yet knowing he had to move, Brazos groped a disbelieving hand along the hot ache that seemed to paralyze his thigh. Realizing then he was cut off briefly from Lambeth's view, he struggled blindly to his feet. His leg nearly buckled; he clamped a hard hand on his thigh and braced his leg stiff and lunged down the hillside in long, floundering strides. He heard Lambeth's wild shout.

The numb thought came to him that Lambeth, having the use of both legs, would overhaul him quickly. He broke his run with his heels and cut left into the trees at an abrupt angle. He went a few more lurching steps and fell on his haunches, hugging the rough bark of a huge pine. He shut his eyes, mastering himself against the cruel life throbbing in his leg. Lambeth's running steps thudded down the slope, and opening his eyes Brazos saw him go past yards away, cuddling his arm, before the trees cut him off.

Brazos forced himself to his feet, his brain darkening with a spasm of pain as he came fully erect. He clung, shuddering, to the trees for long seconds, hearing only the shallow labor of his breathing. Then as sight and sound washed back, he caught drifting shouts from below. He knew what it meant, and he had to move now or be found.

Holding his leg and digging in his heels he began the long descent, clinging where he could to the undergrowth. He reached the bottom dizzy and panting and sank to a crouch behind a bank of shrubbery that ended the timber. From here was a fair view of the bunkhouse where Lambeth's crisp-barked orders were dispersing the crew toward the outbuildings.

He thinks I got that far, Brazos thought, and felt a stir of hope. Lambeth was pulling them away from the house, and his horse was tied by the veranda. If he skirted the house on their blind side to reach the front and the blue, he would still be fully exposed in a dash across the yard. Afoot in the timber he could make his break unseen, but the notion had a suicidal quality: half-crippled and losing blood, he'd be overhauled sooner or later, and he could expect no mercy from John Lambeth.

The Nugget owner hadn't seen DeVries pulling down on his back, only Brazos firing the shot which unknown to him had saved his life. And believing that Pinto had seen and followed them to give his employer a hand if necessary, Lambeth would assume that it was Pinto who, by pulling Brazos' attention had saved him, and in effect died for him. In the savage irony of it, Brazos further knew that by shooting on the two-count he had fully confirmed his nature in Lambeth's eyes, while he would write off that Brazos had not shot to kill as simply bad shooting. With Pinto dead by his hand, Lambeth would not be persuaded otherwise; even if Velez and others of the crew took his side, Lambeth would spare no effort to see him pay.

Grimly weighing it, Brazos did not hesitate now. He left cover and angled across the backyard at a hobbling half-run, reached the corner of the house and worked toward the front hugging the wall, ducking low beneath the windows. His grip was clammy around his gun, he might have to use it again before he was out of this, and in the fury of desperation now, knew that he would. He edged his eyes around the front corner and swept the yard. The men were flung out across the working area in a search of the buildings, and this was the time to move.

He lunged to the tie rail, teeth clamping his lip to keep from crying out at the fire that shot up his leg. It nearly brought him to his knees before he reached the blue and unlooped his reins. He got his good foot into stirrup, and with a tortured effort heaved his hurt leg across the cantle. For agonizing seconds, as his brain blacked from the pain, he had to dredge up a mighty effort to hold himself in saddle.

It was Lila Mae's shrill cry that brought his head up, and she was standing in the doorway two yards away. The fragile softness of her face was erased by a pale and distorted rage, and now she wheeled back into the parlor. Brazos turned the blue and lifted him into a slow trot across the yard, heading upvalley. And as the first warning shout told him he was seen, roweled into a run. A slug kicked up dust to his near right, followed by the roar of a big-caliber rifle; he twisted in his saddle and saw Lila Mae Lambeth on the veranda, frantically levering in another shell as she braced her frail body against a post to shoot again.

The men came boiling out of the buildings, and Stu Sholto,

lumbering in the lead, brought his rifle up on the run. It was plainly no accident that Simon Jack, running almost alongside, suddenly tripped him up with an outthrust foot, Sholto's momentum carrying him butt over teakettle. He heard Lila Mae's rifle roar again. Now Charley Starr was ahead of the others, doggedly firing on the run. Brazos saw him drop to one knee and grab his wrist to steady the gunhand.

Brazos flattened against the blue's mane with a straining urgency as he neared the tack barn, now hearing Charley open up again and the slugs boom into the shiplap planks of the barn. And then he reached its far corner and veered hard, and was cut off from the yard.

He gave the blue its head in a straight southward dash across the open valley toward the frowning ridges that boxed its flank. The hulks of the Diablos, purpled by deep twilight, sprawled away beyond the south basin rim, and the instinct of a hunted man drove him that way. A good flat mile of valley floor was behind him before he looked back, seeing the strung-out line of riders against the windy waves of undulant grass, not close yet coming fast.

His leg was savaged by every hammering thrust of the blue's run, and against it his mind reached for the salve of slow oblivion; he fought the feeling in panic, knowing that here lay the real, the immediate danger. Already the gray seep of dusk was blanketing the land, and if he could hold his saddle for a little, darkness would end first pursuit. Ahead was the cover of the deep foothills, and by the aid of moonlight he could lie up and tend his wound. *Suppose you make it that far, then what?*

His trouser leg was drenched with the hot wetness starting to pool in his boot, and forcing his fingers to explore the long torn muscle of his thigh, he thought the wound to be deep and bad, but the bone seemed untouched. He was losing blood fast as he'd feared, and no help for that till full dark and the rough country above the valley turned back the pursuit.

Where the heights began, he drove the blue up a shallow notch and felt it stumble in the growing dusk. Then, hauling up on a tight rein, he made out the dim outline of a slide where the rimrock had crumbled, and pushed up it, feeling the loose shale give way in a rattling cascade. He turned south along the rim, and seeing the veined shadows that marked a maze of coulees, swung that way. His body was crawling with clammy sweat, his breath a clutching rasp in

73

his lungs; he could hold this pace no longer and must find cover now.

Brazos dropped blindly off the lip of the first gorge, hearing the blue give a panicked snort and brace stiff-legged as the dry cutbank crumbled to its descent into unknown shadow. Its shoes rang on a pebbly bottom and the blue halted, trembling. Brazos started a vague and mechanical move to dismount, then sank back. He might never get back on his feet, and he'd have difficulty enough climbing his mount out of this maze. He closed his eyes and settled his chin to his chest, listening above the sick throb of his head and leg.

Presently he heard the riders clatter up the scarp and onto the rimrock, and they were close by as they halted, talking in mutters. He made out Lambeth's voice, and Velez' too, but not their words. The talk broke off, and he heard their horses move off, turning back.

Brazos sat for long minutes in the shadowed silence, mustering strength and thought as he waited for the moon to show him a way out of this steep-walled gorge. Sluggishly he considered his pumping wound; he reached for a thick branch of scrub fir and tried to break it off. He was weak as a child, and finally he drew his claspknife, opened the blade with his teeth and laboriously sawed through the branch. He cut off a short length and took out his pocket bandanna, tied it around his thigh above the wound, thrust in the stick and twisted it tight. That, by relieving the pressure from time to time, would hold him a while. The bleeding could not be stanched until he was offsaddle and not moving.

The reprieve of darkness eased his danger only a little. He could afford a few hours of rest, then gamble on his seasoned toughness to hold him in the saddle till he'd gained some distance. If he were to lay up here till tomorrow, there were men on the Nugget crew who could track him down in short order. Even so, he had a bleak foretaste of how it would end. The blue had been hard-worked and run hard, and its rider was in worse shape. A half day at the most, before he was overhauled, then be forced to a fighting stand against men of whom only three could be considered enemies. Lambeth himself was at worst a fool, and a gray distaste for the idea filled him, with it a sense of weary defeat.

Unbidden then he remembered Raquel O'Brien's words, *To help one of us makes you the friend of all*. But that thought snubbed against the memory of her father's harsh antagonism.

74

Mike O'Brien, by his own word, would be disposed to shoot him on sight.

He thought of Pepe Garcia, that tough prideful gnome of a man, half-loyal to the sheltering arm of Montalvo but still his own man, running his own sheep. With his help and knowledge of the country, it might be possible to manage a secure hideaway. Pepe was the kind to help the man who had helped him without question or hesitation, and Lambeth being the sort of man he was, any danger of retaliation against Pepe's little family could be safely discounted. What he could not discount was the danger of his untended wound, nor that Pepe's shack was not over a mile distant, easily located by moonlight.

Now, as the early moon shed its first pale hue across the tortured landscape, Brazos pushed up the gorge in a westerly direction, moving carefully through the ground shadows between the walls where the soft high rays did not yet penetrate. Soon the cutbanks shallowed and became less steep, and he climbed the blue out in one driving lunge. He took his bearings by highlighted landmarks, and took up a plodding way due southwest.

His head jounced limply on his chest; the fire that racked his leg ate into his brain with a steady fever. A part of his will, detached, guided his sweating hands on the reins, but shortly he was giving the horse its own head. As a man in fever did, he fixed on one thought and turned it over aimlessly—over and over again: *All that was rigged to get Lambeth killed.*

She had known how he would react to a man's insulting his wife and how he would have to settle it; and however it came out, DeVries would be there to make sure of them both. The shots would fetch the whole crew—ten witnesses to vouch that the two men had killed each other. But Lambeth had plainly been the sure target, for DeVries had aimed at the wounded rancher while Brazos was still unhit. From his wounding Lambeth, DeVries had likely judged him a bad shot, *or he'd have gone for me first.* It was an easy mistake, for few men who worked horses and cattle were more than sorry shucks with the pistols they packed as a matter of course. They were unwieldy close-quarter weapons on which a man burned a lot of costly powder to gain any proficiency.

DeVries hadn't known that a rootless boyhood spent in wild and lonely places, following a trouble-prone old drunk like Pop Melaven, had made Brazos totally dependent on his

75

own eyes and hands. At fourteen he had surprised a camp robber, given him his chance, and shot him dead. To which Pop Melaven had said, cussing him out, *Someday your goddam soft streak is gonna get you killed, boy.* Not so soft, considering that three others had crowded luck with him the same way, and if two of them had lived, it was by that same luck. You could make merciful allowance, though, to a fair-play fool like John Lambeth.

DeVries was Starr's man, means her and Starr were likely together in that. Only for what?

The numb drift of his thoughts went over it again and again in a monotonous treadmill of mounting fever. The slow-pacing blue halted twice, and moved on to the sullen urge of his heels; more than twice he caught himself slipping sideways. He gripped the horn and bowed his face against the blue's mane, and plodded endlessly on. He had the vague thought that since they had spent a night at the Garcia place, the animal might follow the windowlight in. He could no longer lift his head to tell, and was almost past caring.

A man's sharp call—*"Quien es?"*—shocked some of the fog from his mind, and he raised his head, seeing the light stream from an open doorway where a man stood. The words *"Quien es"* came again, now with the softness of dawning recognition, and he tried to answer, and with the effort felt his last strength give. Falling sideways, he lost it all in welcome blackness.

CHAPTER TEN

"JA, ONE ONLY for the road," said Dr. Heimholtz, accepting a glass of brandy. Lila Mae handed the other glass to Lambeth. He was on the settee, propped by pillows, his arm swathed in thick bandages. He promptly tossed off his drink, and the doctor eyed him sternly over his spectacles. "Ha. And one only for you, young man, so peaked and pale."

"Used to the stuff."

"So, so. From the look, you are too used to it. The laudanum I leave, if pain comes, use. If bad it gets, for Heimholtz send. Plenty of the sleep and rest, and the dressings change daily. In a week I will come by." Dr. Heimholtz closed his bag briskly, clamped on his derby, and nodded brusquely to the room at large. Lila Mae let him out, said thanks and a goodbye, and watched him climb into his buggy. She turned back into the room as Sheriff Keogh cleared his throat quietly. He was seated in a worn leather chair, balancing his hat on his crossed knees. He took his brandy, set down his glass and wiped his mustaches with his finger.

"Another drink, sir?"

Keogh's gaze touched her briefly, impersonal as a lizard's. "No, ma'am, thank you kindly."

"Another one, honey?"

Lambeth nodded, handing her his glass to be freshened, and she put her back to both men and walked to the cabinet. Lila Mae let her lip curl faintly as she poured the drink. Last night he had pooh-poohed his wound, letting her clean it and affix a crude dressing; he could see a doctor tomorrow. By early dawn, tossing with restless pain, he had told her to send a man to town. As a matter of spite she had roused Velez himself from his bed, but the foreman hadn't given so much as a disgruntled word. He had made a fast trip, returning with Dr. Heimholtz and the sheriff too. Heimholtz had probed the inflamed and swollen flesh to find the bullet deeply lodged against the bone. John, already fortified by his customary pain-killer, had borne the bloody operation with a white-faced stoicism. *Aren't you the little man though*, she

77

gibed silently, handing him his drink with a smile of wifely concern.

"Mr. Lambeth, you feel up to talking a while?"

"Certainly, sheriff. Though I hardly sent for you, you know. Ramon's idea."

"Take sort of an interest in this kind of business," Keogh observed dryly, reaching in his coat pocket. He brought out a tobacco pouch and a stubby pipe, which he began to pack. "Your permission, ma'am?"

Lila Mae gave him a bright little nod, her face composed as she took a chair and folded her hands on her lap. It could have gone far worse if chance had not allowed John's mistaken interpretation of things, and DeVries' killing she could dismiss with brittle indifference; his sort was nothing but gun and cocky nerve, cheaply bought. But his death had solved nothing. John was alive, and so was Brazos Kane. And Keogh was in it now, thanks to John's greaser foreman. Obliquely she watched Keogh's face as he listened to John.

"That's it, I should say. We lost him by the south ridges as it turned dark, so we came back with the intention of taking up the trail at first light. I rather think that leg of his will slow him down considerably."

"Like enough." Keogh puffed reflectively on his pipe. "Lucky for you Velez brought me before first light. Maybe I can keep you out of a jackpot of trouble."

"Trouble?"

"Kind a man fetches on himself making his own law."

Lambeth flushed, shifting restively against the pillows. "Pinto was in my employ," he said stiffly. "In a way I'm to blame for the poor fellow's death. If he hadn't tried to help me . . ."

"Interesting, that." Keogh leaned forward, settling his elbows on his knees; he stabbed his pipestem gently at the air. "Way you tell it allows that Pinto threw down on Kane. Man defended himself, wouldn't you say?"

Lambeth's color deepened. "I suppose, in a sense, yes. But with Kane about to finish me, Pinto saved my life in doing so."

"If you'll pardon my speaking blunt, that duel was a damnfool thing. Under the circumstances most men wouldn't give him that much chance, and not a jury in the West'd convict a man for killing a drifter who assaulted his wife. Good lawyer might get Kane off for killing DeVries, but he'd have old Nick's own time keeping a rope off his neck for trying to force his way on a woman." Keogh drew absently on his

78

pipe, his eyes narrowed in thought. "Western man who'll molest a woman is a mighty seldom thing. But there's something about that bothers me."

Lila Mae felt a quick stab of wariness, and she said in a light and bantering way, "Why sir, you wouldn't call me a liar?"

"Surely not, ma'am." Keogh smiled, the sun-wrinkled skin at the corners of his eyes crinkling. "Was thinking about how I met Kane. He dropped in on me a while back to ask about a man he was on the hunt for. This man killed an old boy who was Kane's partner, raised him from a tad. Made off with twelve thousand dollars the old fella had on him from selling a lot of horses. Man like Kane just had to look him up, and he'd about nailed him down to the Two Troughs country." Keogh paused, lowering his eyes to his pipe-bowl. "Had it in his head you might be his man, Mr. Lambeth."

Lambeth, speechless for a moment, blurted, "That's absurd!"

"Way I figured," Keogh agreed. "No tie-in but a description he had of the killer from a bartender. But if Kane settled to his own mind that you was his man, he might have molested your wife to prod you to a play. A man crazy for revenge can do odd things."

"I see," Lambeth said slowly, and Lila Mae let her breath out slowly, but the cold worry remained. Keogh was a fair-minded lawman; when and if he caught up with Kane, he would give the other side a fair hearing. And as sheriff, Keogh was in a position to check back the past of Lila Mae Lambeth, genteel wife of a gentleman rancher. That would take letters and time, but eventually he'd learn that she and Charley Starr, Pinto DeVries' partner, had run an Albuquerque casino together, till the city fathers had closed them down. This would prove nothing in itself, *but suppose he told John?*

She had covered that part of her past with a fiction concerning her years as a poor but virtuous seamstress in the anonymity of another large city before coming to New Orleans. This, proven a lie, would cause the whole elaborate illusion she had built for John to shred relentlessly apart, no matter how well she dissembled. She could not afford that, not when failure of one attempt to rid herself of an unwanted husband meant postponing another try indefinitely. Another attempt on John's life now, particularly if Keogh's suspicions were aroused by what Kane could tell him, was out of the question.

"I'll borrow Simon Jack for a day or so, if you've no objection," the sheriff was saying. "A mustanger like Kane will know how to cover his tracks. The Pima's taken county pay more than once, following cold trail for me."

"By all means," Lambeth agreed. "There's the cook's triangle now; he'll be at breakfast. Why don't you eat with the crew, and tell Coosie I said to pack some sandwiches for you."

"Obliged." Keogh rose, and so did Lila Mae, accompanying him to the door.

"I swan, but it's a warm day. I surely don't envy you, having to hunt down that Kane devil in all this heat."

"For a fact, ma'am. Good morning."

Lila Mae closed the door behind him. As she moved back to her chair, Lambeth stirred on the settee and winced, his pale face beaded with sweat. "Could you—"

"Surely." This time she brought the whole decanter from the cabinet, set it at his elbow and watched him pour a large slug. She went to her chair and sat and stared unseeingly at a faded lithograph on the far wall. Just how much of a danger did Brazos Kane pose? She considered carefully. If Kane's wound hadn't been too serious, he would simply ride on from the Two Troughs country, as far and fast as possible. What else could he do, with a charge like attempted rape hanging over him?

On the other hand, if too badly hurt, Kane could be forced to lay up somewhere in the hills. In that case Keogh might hunt him down in short order, with that damned Indian on the track. And then, abruptly, she remembered that it was Simon Jack who had followed Kane's lead in stopping Charley and DeVries when they'd touched off the shooting fracas with two Montalvo men; again, she had seen the Pima working in company with Kane when she had waited to catch him alone to inflict a whipmark. That siwash was Kane's good friend, and almost certainly he would throw Keogh off the scent. Still she would prefer to see Keogh pulled off the hunt for sure. . . .

Her fingers drummed the arm of her chair with a soft excitement, and suddenly she wanted to laugh aloud. Of course there was a way, so obvious she hadn't seen it—and now she was only remotely thinking of Brazos Kane. John had said he wouldn't make a move against Montalvo for no reason, hadn't he? Then give him a reason; let O'Brien provoke John, and not the other way around. And Keogh would have his hands full trying to stop what would follow. . . .

Lambeth was reaching for the third-empty decanter again, and she thought coldly, *No more of that, my friend. Your head has to be clear for this work.* She rose and walked to the settee, gently taking the decanter from him with a misty smile. "Honey, I know it hurts. But please, no more. You've been drinking way too much." There was high color in her face, but he would never guess its cause, as she leaned to him and brushed her lips over his, whispering, "For me, hm?"

How easy it was with him, she thought shutting her eyes to the instant ardor of his embrace; how easy it always was. She panted, arching her breasts to his hands, twisting her face and neck unceasingly as he covered them with kisses. "Oh honey, honey, it's been such a while—" She felt his sharp wince. "There . . . I'm hurting you. So sorry."

He shook his head, his eyes shining. "I didn't feel a thing, my dear."

CHAPTER ELEVEN

THE FIRST THING he became aware of was the trickle of water, and he sluggishly forced his eyes open. The darkness around him was solid and formless with a wash of gray light at one edge. He set his teeth and turned his head by inches, now seeing the jagged patch of false dawn that was a cave mouth. The anonymous shape of a man squatted on his heels there, arms crossed on his knees, and Brazos made a husking sound.

"Senor?"

"Pepe?"

"Yes," Pepe Garcia said. "Rest easy." He picked up a canteen that was Brazos' own and stood, shaking out the thick wool poncho bunched around his shoulders. He moved deeper into the cave and hunkered by the wounded man. There was enough light to pick up the blur that was a grin on his ugly gnome's face. "This is a place I know, a cave. It is hid good. You are hunted for?"

Brazos grunted.

"This, Pepe figure. I made a travois and fix it to your horse, bring you here while it is dark, and pull you up to this cave on a rope. It is rough for your hurt, but to do this before daylight was good. Then they will come, eh?"

Brazos lay quietly on his back, feeling the thick pallet of blankets under his back, his hips contoured into the soft sand floor. He felt the dismal ache of his leg, and did not try to shift about. His lips barely stirred with the effort of speech. "Could be trouble, Pepe."

"Hell," Pepe snorted. "This is Montalvo land, but deep in the hills. Here is nothing but badlands, rock and brush. Who will trail here?"

"I mean for you."

"My place too is inside Montalvo line. So far men will come, but they will be careful about coming farther, which might make trouble. And they will not hurt a woman or a baby, though my Juana and my Luis will be gone anyway if they come. But your enemy, they are men from Nugget ranch maybe?"

"A long story, Pepe."

"Then it will wait. Will you have a drink?" Pepe tilted

the canteen to his lips, and Brazos drank a little. Pepe went on cheerily: he had told his young wife to pack a few necessities, and while moonlight held, to take herself and the baby to Montalvo headquarters and the house of her parents, Armando and Pilar Pesquiera, and tell her father to bring certain necessary supplies to this cave. Juana would remain at her parents' for a few days, as if on an ordinary visit. Should Brazos' enemy trail him to the Garcia place meantime, they would find an empty house and a cold hearth. They could follow the litter track Pepe had left but a short distance, and the trail would peter away on bare rock. He had chosen a devious path through the badlands, which he knew like the face of his mother, to reach this cave, of which few people knew.

"I'm sorry for this, Pepe. I came to your home over terrain that'll be hard to track—may throw 'em off. But this is hard on you and her."

Pepe's snort deprecated the notion. "Juana is strong as a she-mule; the baby is fat and sound. A few miles' walk did not hurt them, and the country there is open and easy. By now she is safe with her mama, and Armando is on his way. You will not be moving a while; you will need grub and medicine, eh? Of doctoring, except for the sheep, I am a fool, and we had nothing but clean cloth and hot water. I did my best, but Armando will know what to do. The Pesquieras will keep this quiet, so Senor Mike does not know. It's said he passed hard words with you once, so that is best."

"My horse?"

"I turned him into a side canyon close by here where is good grass and a spring. I put on his hobble and strung your rope across the way to keep him in."

Brazos fumbled a cautious hand along his thigh; a slight probing touch shuddered a wrenching ache through his leg. Clammy sweat started on his body as he felt carefully the bulky rough bandage, and the fresh warm soaking of it. Quiet as he was, there was some bleeding. He stilled a nudge of cold panic, settled his muscles to a forced relaxing.

"You will sleep more, eh?" Pepe said. "I watch for Armando."

He returned to his squatting vigil at the cave mouth, and Brazos closed his eyes against the chill burn of fever behind them. Before long it would be worse, much worse, and despite Pepe's assurances he regretted having to embroil him and others in his trouble. Now too, with his fever low and his head still clear, he tasted the bitter possibility that by

83

involving even Pepe Garcia with his latitude of independence from Montalvo proper, he might have provided the friction that would spark off the growing tension between Montalvo and Nugget. Even if Lambeth could trail him no farther than Pepe's shack, he would know the truth, and if he had the bad judgment to carry the search to O'Brien himself . . . no good thinking about it. Now, there was nothing to do but wait.

The gurgle of running water somewhere outside the cave was a refrain to his drowsy thoughts; he dozed to its lulling chuckle and presently woke once more, now to the thin clamor of a shod horse crossing rock, somewhere below the cave. Pepe was on his feet, hands cupped to his mouth, and he called a soft halloo.

The clean young light of full dawn was streaming into the cave now, and Brazos saw that a vaulting wall of granite, eroded and crumbling, faced its mouth. The floor of the cave jutted out to a narrow lip of rock, then appeared to end in a clean drop-off. Though he could not see its rim-rock, he guessed that the far wall was the near-vertical flank of a steep canyon, and that the cave penetrated into its opposite side, well above the canyon floor. This place must be deep in the south basin ridges where they abutted against the Diablos, and its feel of lonely seclusion real enough. He heard the rider's dismount, and a moment later his scrambling ascent of the rugged canyon wall.

Pepe's sharp, "Careful, senorita," gave him a start, and so did the sight of Raquel O'Brien as Pepe reached down to catch her arm, assisting her onto the narrow ledge. She paused to peer against the cave's gloom, and she made a small sturdy shape against the dawnlight. She dropped the bulky tarp-wrapped bundle she carried, then sank down beside it to catch her breath.

Pepe said uneasily, "It is not so good, Miss Raquel, for you to come here. *Caramba!* This wife of mine, she is a great fool at times."

"Calm yourself, Pepe. This was no doing of Juana's. Pilar Pesquiera came to my room and woke me; she and Armando do not keep medical supplies or a lot of food in their little 'dobe. There was a need, she said, and I made her tell me. Then I insisted on coming myself."

"It is not right," Pepe said stiffly. "The daughter of the patron—"

Raquel laughed softly and made a wide arc with her hand. "Look. This canyon, this cave. Do you remember, Pepe,

84

how we all played here as children, and were we as peon and patroness then?"

Pepe, for whom some things were ordained and unalterable, muttered an obscure "Si" and began to open the pack. She climbed to her feet and stumbled as she moved to Brazos' side, kneeling by him. He shook his head feebly.

"You are our friend," she said simply. "Didn't I say so?"

"Pepe is right."

"Pepe can be wrong," she said with tart impatience. "So can other men. Lie still if you can." Her hands were moving carefully, undoing the clotted bandage. Brazos half-raised his head, ignoring the fresh start of pain in the shock of seeing his upper leg. The pants leg had been cut away above the wound and the flesh, mangled and swollen where the bullet had emerged, was caked by dark and drying blood which stiffened his trousers and puddled the blanket under his leg. New blood welled bright and angry from the exposed hole.

There was not a faint tremor in the olive smoothness of her face or in her hands, working deftly and steadily. She dropped the bloody mess of tangled wrappings to one side, then settled on her heels and studied the wound. She said without turning her head, "Pepe. Will a fire be safe?"

"Si, I can build her with 'most no smoke."

"Do that." She rose briskly, and went to the articles which Pepe had spread out on the tarp, while he vanished nimbly over the ledge. She had packed abundant grub supplies, and she piled these neatly to one side as she sorted out a small pot, a length of stiff wire, salve, bluestone, sweet oil, and strips of a clean and silky material that might have been salvaged from discarded unmentionables. There was also a bottle wrapped in a flour sack. She unwrapped it, pulled the cork with her teeth, and spilled a tin cup half-full and carried it to him.

"I never thought I should be giving a man whiskey." Her smile did not touch the dark gravity of her gaze. She knelt again, held up his head as he drank. "More?"

He nodded, steeling himself against the liquor's reaching fire before he spoke. "You plan on cauterizing it?"

She was on her feet, half-turning, and now she paused gravely. "Yes. I'll soak a rag in whiskey and run it through with a wire. Then heat the ramrod of Pepe's rifle . . . well . . . you'd better take all the whiskey you can."

Brazos found himself remembering as clearly as yesterday another burning. When he had been briefly farmed out to a

85

strict and penurious uncle after his parents' death, the old man had one day caught him pilfering out of the sugar jar with a wet thumb and, to show him the error of his ways, had held the offending hand on a hot stovelid. The excruciating memory still touched him with a nameless horror, and all he could think was, *don't let her see it.*

He took a second half-cup of whiskey, and then Pepe returned with an armload of dead brush. The fever and the drink made a tipsy blur of his thoughts; his flesh felt pleasantly numb except for the memory-scorching of his right hand, and he only laughed at it. "He is getting wild now, and he may fight," he heard Pepe say from a long distance off. "We had better get this over quick." A slow flare of firelight flooded the gloomy walls, and he had the illusion of dancing flames all around. He thrashed feebly and shouted his panic, but whether aloud or in his mind he never knew. Strong hands clamped his shoulders, and he ceased to fight. He watched in fascination the red-glowing ramrod take form and move toward him, and someone said, "Hold tight," as the ramrod came down. His muscles strung hard against the heat that seemed to sear his eyeballs; his groin and guts were on fire and his mind reached for the cool blackness that swept over him.

Consciousness came slowly, like a gentle hand stroking across his body; when he tried to move, he knew a terrifying weakness, as if his bones had gone to water. His eyelids were heavy as lead, but when he forced them open things came to clear and instant focus. His mind was clear too, except for a residue of fever throbbing in his temples. He found himself bundled to the chin with thick blankets, sweating profusely, and a scorching thirst ravaged his gullet.

He turned his head cautiously. The sun was high, he knew from the shimmer of heat along the canyon wall. Raquel sat sideways to him in the entrance, her hands clasped around her updrawn knees, looking out. The sunlight glowed softly along the curve of her cheek, and her profile was serene as a dark madonna's. The hidden stream trailed its clear chuckle into the midday silence.

Brazos weakly stirred a hand beneath the blankets, touching his leg. He found it bulky with loosely tied silk, and except for a steady ache like a remote and angry toothache, there was no pain. His mind flinched, remembering the redhot iron; it must have been Pepe who held him and she who . . . He watched her with a silent wonder. She was a gently-bred girl with an unexpected reserve of toughness that was gentle too. His thought veered automatically to Lila Mae Lambeth, and he knew at once that there was no comparison. Yet it must be a common thing with their sex, that at bottom each was iron-tough in her own way, and he felt a drowsy astonishment that few men ever realized so simple a fact. It was men who wove their insipid fictions around women, and most women compounded the folly by believing them. Others like Lila Mae turned them to calculating advantage, and a few like Raquel O'Brien simply ignored them.

His parched lips made a croaked-whisper sound. "Water." She picked up the canteen and brought it to him, her hands tender beneath his head as she tilted it and he drank greedily. Water had never tasted better, and it was cool from resting against a large rock out of the sun. With the edge off his thirst, he was conscious of the strength of her hands and the faint clean smell of her.

"Not too much . . . there." She capped the canteen and set it near his hand. Kneeling close, she stripped two of the blankets off him and folded them by his feet. "Better?"

"Yes'm, thanks."

She settled on her hips, tucking her legs beneath her and leaning on one hand, the other smoothing the worn riding skirt over her thigh. The half-smile was on her lips, now touching her dark gaze. "You were shaking with chills, then burning up. We had to keep you warm. But I think the fever has about burned itself out. How do you feel?"

"Reckon all right, considering this morning—"

"My friend, this morning was yesterday. Pepe left to see to his sheep, and when I left late in the day, he was back to spend the night with you. And I'm back for today."

He wriggled uncomfortably, feeling a sudden acute embarrassment. "Ma'am, I am surely thankful. It ain't . . . wasn't as though you owed me a thing."

"Sometimes men are fools," she observed tartly. "There's a brave kind of pride, and a foolish kind too. How can a man think that he can do a good thing for one's friends and expect less in return? I said you were our friend, but if you wish to call it payment—call it a debt that is paid."

"Didn't mean it that way," he muttered. "Only this is nothing for someone like you to be mixed up in. You could have let Pesquiera come . . ."

"Yes, someone like me, someone so different. Pepe can't help thinking as he does, but on you, an Anglo so proud and be-damned-to-all, such talks sets poorly. I quit school in the

East to be a nurse in a hospital, and when my father found out, he ordered me home. When I wouldn't come, he came for me. And I came then because I saw I'd hurt him."

Sometimes, Brazos thought wryly, his habit of taciturnity was a useful thing. He said nothing, grinning.

"So you think it's funny?"

"No."

She drew her knees up and settled her chin on them, her gaze so darkly brooding it discomfited him. "You have a way about you that's easy not to like."

"I reckon."

"Listen. Someone can be born what they are and have the hunger for more. A hunger for what? For blood, for dirt and sweat? Perhaps I'm the foolish one. But these things are the lot of nearly all people on this earth, and I think that knowing them is all that makes us, the few lucky ones, human. My father knows this; he lives it. Why should he expect his only child to be different?"

She was a strange girl, at once childlike and possessing a sure wisdom that came to most women in middle life or later, and he knew, if he'd also known how to give it tongue, the aching and indefinable hunger she meant. "Well," he said after a lame moment, "this was an ugly job for anyone. Hope I didn't get too mean."

She gave him a carefully oblique look. "Well—you talked."

He said warily, "Oh."

"About many things," she nodded slowly. "Sometimes quietly, sometimes in a rage so we had to hold you down. Most of it is pretty clear, and the rest I can guess." She reached for his hand, and turned it palm upward, touching the tracery of old scars. "This is the hand you didn't want to get burned again."

"Other scars," he said surlily. "That was a long time ago."

"Yes, a good many scars ago." She dropped his hand to the blanket, her face almost fiercely grave. "What have you ever had, Brazos Kane, besides the name of a river?"

"We had a life of sorts, me and Pop Melaven, not much a one by most accounting."

"No. This man you call Pop, I think he had you. And whatever he gave you, he took back many times over. And you only a boy. Then what did you have? And what have you lost?" She swung to her feet, her eyes stormy. "I don't know that we did you any favor, Pepe and I. You have a fine empty life that you want to fill with revenge."

88

He watched her with a mild wonderment. "You want to sit down?"

"No, I don't want to sit down," she mimicked him furiously, and stalked to the goods spread out on the tarp. "These things I wasted time bringing will keep you for a while. Plenty of food, tobacco too, and there is a clear stream outside. You needn't want for water. You can do your cooking at night, when the smoke will not be seen." Her toe gave a box an angry nudge. "Here is stuff for your hurt. A strong man like you, needing nothing and surely not us, can change his own bandages. Would you like more shells for your gun? You have a man to kill, I believe. Would you like to know that the sheriff is looking for you?" She paused scathingly, hands on her hips. "Have I missed anything? Anything at all, if you can bring yourself to ask?"

Brazos said nothing for a moment, wondering what she was angry about. "One thing I was sort of wondering."

"By all means."

"Can you whisper?"

She folded her arms glaring, and turned her back and faced stiffly out toward the hot canyon. "Yes, I can whisper. What do you want to know?"

After telling her as much as he thought worthwhile, he asked about the search for him and learned that Sheriff Keogh, having apparently put down Lambeth's hunt for him, was scouring the basin for him with Simon Jack Pima. Raquel eyed him suspiciously.

"What is so funny?"

"Nothing. Just Simon Jack's a friend of mine."

Simon Jack was a Pima, and even the Apaches respected those wily trackers. He was probably the one man who could do the job for Keogh, and since the search was already two days old, it could only mean that Simon Jack was using every trick at his command to throw the sheriff off the true scent. Eventually, unless he saw through the subterfuge, Keogh would conclude in disgust that his quarry had made a clean escape over the mountains.

"I am glad you admit to one friend. In any case, only a few of us who grew up here know of this cave. The opening cannot be seen from the trail, and you will hear anyone who comes." Her eyes crinkled quizzically at the corners. "One of our vaqueros met the sheriff and the Pima yesterday, north by the breaks. Keogh is questioning everyone, and he tells them that you . . . well, attacked Mrs. Lambeth. Does your taste run to such pale little things?"

"I told you how that was," Brazos growled, nettled. She might not understand that it was no laughing matter, that he was in deep trouble if he were caught before, somehow, he could clear his name. On a woman's word in such a matter, any cow-country jury would have him hung. It would be suicidal to tell his story to the sheriff without proof. No matter how fair a lawman Keogh was, he was also a Texan; as one of the breed himself Brazos knew that on such a charge he could look for no help there. To pull his head out of the noose, he needed to learn the truth of the hidden game being played out by the fine hand of Lila Mae Lambeth. He needed someone who could not only be trusted and who would trust his word against Lila Mae's but who was in a position to do him some good.

To his question, Raquel said unhesitatingly, "Yes, Bernardo Velez, Ramon's cousin, is with our crew. He can get Ramon word, and Pepe can bring Ramon here."

"Good." He looked at her carefully. "If I can say something and not make you mad, best thing you can do for me after that is not come here again."

"Meaning I could be watched and followed?"

"So could Pepe or Ramon. But you're a woman."

"Oh, well, and a stupid woman would surely lead the sheriff straight here."

Brazos gave her a glance of dour perplexity, and shook his head. "I told you about Charley Starr. He's tied in this somehow with her, with Mrs. Lambeth. I don't know much about that, but just enough to worry them. If they get a notion you know something, it could be rough. Velez has a stake in this, and Pepe'll have to watch his back anyway; they'll know I helped him once, and it could occur to them he might have helped me. No need for you to put your head on the block."

She was silent for a moment, and then with total irrelevance: "What kind of a man is John Lambeth?"

"A kind of fool, at worse. His wife . . ."

He did not go on, and Raquel said calmly, "Of course this was a leading question, which I withdraw. I have only seen, never met her. I have never hated anyone either, but I should guess she would be easy to hate." She gave him a slow nod, her eyes flat and guarded. "You think perhaps that you know about women. I doubt that you do."

"The way I recall," he said dourly, "I didn't make claim to."

CHAPTER TWELVE

PEPE RETURNED well before sunset. He'd fetched Raquel's black from the branch canyon where it was picketed, and was holding it saddled and ready as she descended from the cave. She stepped into the saddle, and then said tartly, "I may not be back, Pepe. Do you have a message for Juana?"

"Nothing she does not know." Pepe's ugly face was thoughtful as he studied hers. "That is a very tough man, eh, senorita?"

She felt a slow warmth color her face. "Why do you say that?"

"From how you speak, I think he has come awake and talks tough."

"There was talk." She reined in the fretting black with an irritable hand. "Tomorrow Ramon Velez may come to see you. Bring him here. The tough one will tell you why. Adios."

She pulled the black around and heeled him upcanyon, and shortly left the badlands for the long grassy slopes of Montalvo's southern acres. She set a brisk pace on a northwest beeline for the headquarters, frowning with her thoughts. She wryly wondered why she was forever getting angry about things she could not change. *But that grin of his. If I were a man, I would want to hit him.* Yet she thought with a small shame of her parting words to Kane, "By the way, I also brought you a change of clothes and a razor; you might use them." It was tempting, of course, to gadfly a hard-shelled man obviously unused to a woman's company. But she did wonder what he'd look like minus that fiery scrub of whiskers.

He was an independent, withdrawn and short-spoken man with a go-to-hell insolence about him that deeply provoked her; after he had slept off the dregs of fever and woke again, shortly before Pepe's arrival, she had tried to draw him out. He wouldn't say much, but enough to astonish her with his knowledgeable range of most subjects. He was wholly undisciplined in his breadth of encyclopedic detail and patchwork lack of formal fundamentals, his judgments unanswerably shrewd because they were largely built of hard experience. "I read," had been his terse explanation. "Mostly we wintered alone with nothing but time on our hands. Pop would pack in a couple barrels of whiskey, me a packload of books. No choice—you learned to stretch booze or your mind."

I wonder what we were arguing about, really? A perplexed frown continued to mar her forehead, as she pulled finally onto the brow of hills above the headquarters. It lay cupped in a gently sloping valley under the shelving west foothills, and Raquel drew rein to give the black a breather before taking the last slopes. Since her return from the East, the sight of her ancestral home touched her in a way she hadn't been aware of in girlhood. It wasn't only that in the cities she'd encountered a side of life that had appalled her, cramped and mean and swarming, with a hopeless chasm between rich and poor. Behind all his loudness and bluster, her father knew her mind keenly, and he'd been right, finally, in this: she was part of this land and one with it, bone and blood, and she would not leave it again. She tried to think of Brazos Kane in a city, and she grinned. It was unthinkable.

She crossed the valley at an idle lope, seeing the sunset crown the snowy peaks while their vast shadows crept to meet her. Presently she reached the sprawl of peon's homes below the working area of the headquarters. She dropped off at the Pesquiera 'dobe for a few minutes to chat with Juana and her mother, assured them that Pepe was well and spent a few minutes longer playing with small Luis. Afterward she visited the home of Bernardo Velez to give him Kane's message to Ramon. His wife Maria said that Bernardo was not yet home, and would the senorita wait? Raquel said that she would return later, and took her leave. She rode through the maze of barns and stables and outsheds to reach the corrals, turned the black over to a stableboy, and went on to the house.

The main building of the old Montalvo manor was adobe and two-storied, with a broad stone porch supporting ornate gallery columns and a balcony with a railing of lacework iron. It had a rough magnificence in this country, having been added on to over the generations so that the result was a cross-dog blend of old adobe and newer timber, with the flanking wings angled to enclose stone-flagged patios. Each separate room in the wings had an outside door, so that she was able to enter a patio archway and slip into her own room undetected. It was a relic habit from her childhood when, coming in from a happy day of play with the peon children, she'd found it prudent to bathe and change her soiled frock before braving her father's stern eye. It was still not a bad idea, as wry experience had taught her.

Now as then, her conspirator Sarita, the ancient housekeeper, had a wooden tub and buckets of hot and cold water ready. At exactly fifteen minutes before the supper hour, Sarita silently entered the room on rope-soled sandals, muttered, "Buenas noches," laid a freshly starched dress on the bed and made her noiseless retreat. She slipped into the dress, a white lawn frock with a blue sash and with blue ribbon threading its full sleeves and skirt hem, ran a brush through the dark mass of her hair and ribboned it in a snug knot behind her neck.

She left her room and followed the corridor into the main house, crossing the great cool parlor with its yard-thick walls of whitewashed adobe and broad windows covered with heavy portholed shutters—memento of the days when the Apaches, in the easternmost swing of their raids, had made forays on the blooded horse stock of Montalvo. The furniture was a strange hybrid of Spanish and New England colonial. The adjacent dining room was as large, with a long oak table and handcarved chairs that would seat thirty guests, but it was far from adequate on the holidays when Mike O'Brien threw the big house open to parties and dances, attended by all the Montalvo people.

Raquel paused in the doorway, seeing her father at the head of the long table, wearing his usual careless *charro* attire as he hunched over a tally book. She thought, *he should not read in this light,* and was struck by the lonely picture he made at the empty table in the big room. She had never thought of burly, boisterous Mike as lonely, but in her whole memory there was only the two of them, and his serious moods were gruff and unconfiding. He glanced up now, seeing her, and what seemed like an oath stirred his lips.

She came around the table to him, planted a kiss on his forehead, and took the chair on his right. "Good evening, old bear. *El viejo.*"

"Old one, bedamned," Mike growled, laying aside the tally book as he roared over his shoulder, "Sarita!"

"What a lovable bear. Why did you look at me that way?"

"No reason. You were standing, just so—"

"I know," she smiled. "I look like Mother."

"Which, was I a godly man, I'd thank the Lord for. Sarita!"

The old housekeeper glided silently from the kitchen with a

tray of steaming dishes, and he cocked his head ingratiatingly. "Ah, you Spanish dear, how is it you look more ravishing every evening?"

Sarita shrugged and muttered, *"Loco,"* as she lighted the two thick candles that centered the table and faded into the kitchen again. Mike began to fork food onto his plate with gusto, twitching a dour glance at his daughter. "May I ask where you've been gallivanting all day?"

"Oh, here and there. Now what have I done?" He scowled his reproval, and she sighed and picked up her fork. "All right, I'll be proper and decorous for a while. Since Sarita won't let me lift a finger to ordinary housework, it will be needlework, of course. And preparations for a *baile* or something. All very proper, and all useless."

"Damn." Mike glowered into his cup of black coffee, nursing a scalded tongue. "Don't get bucko with me, miss. You could be turning your mind to a useful enough thing—marriage. By God, giving you your scamp run of the place all those years was only my first mistake; sending you to a mannered school was the second." He snorted an oath. "Manners! All ye picked up was a pack of half-noodled ideas about women's rights and other radical nonsense. If I found you a likely lad, you'd turn around and marry some saddle bum just to spite me."

Raquel folded her hands beneath her chin and half-lowered her lashes. "And what would you do if I did?"

"Call you your father's daughter, for sure," Mike grinned, and frowned again. "I'll tell you. I'd take a buggy whip . . ."

He let his voice trail, his brows scowling as he turned his head. Raquel caught it then, the gathering knot of men's angry voices outside the house. Mike muttered, "Plague the devil," as he rose, balling his napkin; he flung it on his plate and stalked toward the front door. She hurried up behind him as he flung it open, moving onto the porch.

"Here, what's this about?"

From the doorway, Raquel saw the group of mounted men, with John Lambeth and Sheriff Keogh in the lead, pulled watchfully together against the Montalvo vaqueros. A number of them afoot flanked the horsemen, others were coming on the run from the direction of the 'dobes and the bunkhouse. Most of them were armed, as were the Nugget riders, and the fading glare of sunset picked out the tight, restless movement of knife-edged hostility. Something was ready to break here.

"Mike," Liam Keogh called sharply, as Mike came off the porch toward them, "you better slack down now."

"Slack down, is it? I'll give no order to any effect, till you say what this's about." He came to a halt, hands on his hips, his glare sweeping the group. Charley Starr had ranged up by John Lambeth, crowding Ramon Velez' mount aside. Starr sat his saddle with a slack indifference that matched his sleepy gaze, while he quietly usurped the old foreman's place.

"About a bad thing, Mike. Look here," Keogh said turning his horse; the movement broke the group apart. Raquel saw that old Mose Cruikshank and the thick, dull-faced man called Sholto had their ropes dabbed on a fat steer, sidling their ponies to either side to hold the ropes taut. The frightened whiteface's eyes rolled wildly; ropy saliva hung from its mouth as it braced its spread legs against the ropes. Keogh dismounted, motioning to Mike, and the two of them skirted the steer. The sheriff pointed at its glossy flank.

"What would you call that?"

Mike squinted. "A stamp N made over to M with a running iron. They made a fine botch of it."

"They?"

"Whoever done it." Mike straightened up, nestling his thumbs in the sash of his trousers, and his nod at Lambeth held a wicked arrogance. "Likely him."

John Lambeth was sitting his saddle in a half-slump, as if to ease the hurt of his arm, which was in a black silk sling. Now he came swiftly erect, saying hotly, "What? That's a lie!"

"Mr. Lambeth," Keogh said with a mild warning note, "you agreed I'd handle this."

"But dammit, he's not the least surprised! Look at him."

"Now," Mike said with arrogant disdain, "should I be surprised that a man who hires the likes of that—" He nodded at Starr "—has a bit more nasty work in his craw."

"Mike," Keogh said flatly, "no more of that. Lambeth, I'm holding you to your word."

A bit chain rattled in the trailing silence, and a horse gave a slobbering snort. Raquel felt the full rush of angry bewilderment now; what did this mean?

Keogh gently stroked his jaw with his thumb, eying the steer. "Funny thing about this. Six head of Nugget short-horns, prime stuff, way back in Blanco Canyon over northwest —you know the place, Mike?"

"Aye, free range."

Keogh nodded. "Seems this afternoon Sholto and Mose here were ranging the deep brush for any last strays. And found these six, all overbranded alike. How old would you make that running brand?"

Mike said, "A couple days or less," his words coming slow and ominous now. *Please,* Raquel prayed silently, *please let him keep his temper!*

"Same for that earmark, you reckon? I mean the underbit." Keogh pointed at the raw notch in the steer's left ear. "That over-and-underbit of yours is registered in the county brand book. Nugget takes a plain overbit."

Mike coughed deep in his throat, the ruddiness of his sun-boiled face deepened by a kindling wrath. There was a stir of movement among the muttering vaqueros, and Mike chopped it off with a lifted hand. He eyed Keogh with a bitter disbelief. "Why man, do you mean to hear me deny it? Is that it, Liam?"

"I don't need your word on anything, Mike. But I'd like it said out, yes."

"Hellfire! You're well told I'll say it, and to the face of any blackleg lying bastard who says I been rigging another outfit's brands!"

John Lambeth cleared his throat, coldly. "Someone is. How about his riders?"

"Why, I believe the dear lad is calling my people, now." He lifted his arm toward Lambeth, pointing his finger like a gun. "Get this, you whiskey-addled pup. There are no thieves on Montalvo!"

Lambeth's reputed drinking might account for the general conviction, publicly aired, that he was a loose and spineless man. None of the hearsay fitted him now, Raquel thought. He calmly ignored Mike and fitted a stare of cold challenge on the sheriff. "As I understand it," he said coolly, "they hang a man for stealing one horse. How many steers does it take to make a simple arrest?"

Mike said a ripe oath as he started forward, roaring, "By God, I'll break your damned head for that!"

Keogh pivoted around behind him, his lean arms clamped Mike around the chest. "Quit it! Dammit, Mike, quit it now!"

Mike struggled against the pinning hold; he broke it with a strong heave and surged toward Lambeth's horse, his face distorted by fury. Keogh palmed up his gun and took a long step, his arm chopping up and down. The muzzle caught Mike smartly behind the ear, and his knees folded. Without a sound he slumped bonelessly forward, and Keogh caught him and began to ease him down.

Raquel heard a low oath in liquid Spanish, and the brittle

snack of a rifle hammer pulling back. She cried, "No," breaking her moment of unmoving shock. "No, Jaime!" She stumbled in her haste, and caught up her rustling skirt as she came swiftly off the porch.

Jaime Elias' eyes blazed in his young thin face, as his half-raised rifle froze. The vaqueros stood tensed, and she turned a look of desperate appeal on Armando Pesquiera. He was standing ahead of the others, and he passed his dark steady glance over them, one by one. Armando was of an age with Mike O'Brien, his *segundo*, and his reverse in temperament. The others respected his lead. "There will be no gunplay here," he said quietly. "Give me that, Jaime."

Young Elias sullenly passed him the rifle. Raquel dropped to her knees by her father, and Keogh eased him into her arms, then stood erect. He held his drawn gun flat against his thigh, watching only Charley Starr whose hand was flexed over his pistol butt. "Mister, you move that hand again, it better be empty."

John Lambeth said then, his face pinched with anger. "All right, Charley." Starr twitched a bland smile, and shrugged his hand open and let it fall.

"I told you he was no man to bring," Keogh said bitingly.

"Yes, you've told me a good deal, sheriff. I'm getting a bit tired of playing the docile greenhorn that any man can insult or steal from if he takes a mind." He nodded at O'Brien, whose big head lay limp against Raquel's lap. "That man is a mad dog as well as a—"

"Shut your fool mouth," Keogh said with weary disgust, "or what he commenced will get finished. You don't call a man that way unless you hold some smart proof."

"My God, man, what do you need? Those steers—"

"Those steers bedamned! Bad job of doctoring a few brands could mean a bad joke—anything. I'll find out about that. Meantime you'll get your arrest, no help for it now." Keogh's bleak glance found the girl. "Mike won't be a mind to abide any of this when he comes around. You understand? Now, I'll have to take him in."

Raquel did not answer at once. She knew the brutal truth of Keogh's words, and knew too that the decision was hers. With Pesquiera's backing, she could sway the situation here by a word, but only till Mike regained his senses. Yet Keogh's solution quietly appalled her, and she shook her head. "I do see what you mean, but jailing him will only make it worse. I'm sorry."

"So am I, missy," Keogh said somberly. "I have known

97

your pa a sight longer than any man here. A spell in jail might crease some of the starch out of his mick temper. If nothing else, it'll buy some time to find out the truth. I'm asking you to let me have it."

Raquel compressed her lips. When he came to, Mike would be like a wild man, she knew, and beyond that her mind was a stony blank. "But what can you do?"

"I'll put Simon Jack Pima to work hunting for sign in Blanco Canyon. He might find something we missed, though going by the work he's done for me of late, I make it no great prospect." He looked at her squarely. "I'll need a wagon for Mike. He was disturbing the peace."

She looked down at Mike, smoothed the silvered hair along his temple, and felt almost a turncoat's guilt as troubled decision came. *It is for him,* she told herself fiercely, *not for this stupid charge.* She raised her eyes to Pesquiera's searching look and gave him a weary nod. Armando rapped a sharp order, and the crew broke up, two of them heading for the wagon shed.

"I'd say it's open and shut," Lambeth said softly. "I don't like your attitude, sheriff, but I'll settle for your miserable charge—for now."

"Boy," the sheriff said gently, "you got what you wanted. Now you get home to your loving wife and thank the God that made a fool like you for adding a clear streak of luck. Because mister, you had it just now."

Lambeth kicked his horse savagely around and away. After a moment Charley Starr swung after him, and Velez, his seamed face full of a deep trouble, started to follow. "Ramon," Keogh said sharply, and Velez turned. "Ramon, if you have any voice with him, you'd better talk some sense into him."

Quietly, Velez shook his head. "I don't know that the senor will listen to me after today. He has changed, and I am afraid what may come of this."

He said it simply, with a peculiar flatness that thickened the knot of fear in Raquel's throat, and put his horse after Sholto and Mose Cruikshank as the two of them hoorawed the skittish steer back the way they had come. The vaqueros were dispersing slowly, watching the retreating Nugget men with dark and stony faces. Armando Pesquiera moved among them as they straggled off, talking to each with a quiet vehemence, but more than words would be needed to shore up the loyal and fiery pride of these men. Next to a stealer of horses a cow thief was the lowest sort of thing they knew, and they had seen their patron unjustly accused and then humiliated like a dog. They had seen the need, yet did not see it, not when his honor was their own and was dragged in the dust while they were told to hold silent and do nothing.

Raquel O'Brien, knowing each and every man of them, knew she'd committed an almost unpardonable act in siding with the man who had struck down her father. *What else could I do?* Yet what had she done but effect a clumsy stopgap in the smoldering short-fuse of a stiffening hostility, the time she had bought for Keogh useful only while he could hold Mike, which would not be for long. And now John Lambeth, in a fresh turn of temper, had shown a headstrong and violent streak of his own, held in thin abeyance by the sheriff's bold stand. Sinkingly Raquel knew she could do only two things: try to reason with Mike and meantime do her best to keep the aroused vaqueros in check.

She said wearily to Keogh, "I'll ride to Diablo with you. I can talk to him, though I can't hope that it will do any good."

"I'd be obliged if you would. About all anyone can do, and it won't be me he listens to after this."

CHAPTER THIRTEEN

THE EARLY MORNING was cool and bright as the Lambeths crossed the yard toward the corrals. Lila Mae breathed deeply of the crisp air and riffled her curls with a small gloved hand, smiling up at John Lambeth. He saw the pleasure in her eyes; he knew he looked a world better these days, with a clear-eyed and debonair poise about his new-found self. Lately it had been good between them, so good he couldn't believe it would last. *My God,* he thought, *if I were to lose her now . . . what?* Even the thought brought a disquieting qualm, because he knew the answer: it would, to all intent, mark the end of his life.

A loud lift of voices caused him to glance up, frowning. "What the devil's going on?"

As usual the hands were assembled by the corral for their orders, but this morning the line that split them was plain, the regular crew hanging back from Charley Starr and his five imported toughs. Young Jigger Kearny was doing most of the talking, and he was mad.

"Hell, it's past time a man spoke up," he blazed, in answer to a placating word from Ramon Velez. "This place has got higher than a skunkbit hog of late." He laid his hot stare hard against Starr. "I'll take a hand for the outfit hires me, maybe even a fighting one happen they're deserving. But not for no pack of sonofabitching killers."

A mutter of agreement passed through the other regulars. Charley Starr's eyelids drooped with sleepy disdain as he stood at ease, hipshot. He said softly, "Anyone not liking it can haul his freight."

Lambeth strode angrily over to the men. "What in blazes are you fellows about? Jigger, what's the trouble?"

Kearny's young face had gone pale under its deep weathering, but he swiveled a quick, furious stare against John. "I got no trouble, Mr. Lambeth. It's you—you hired it. I got no part in it if I pull out, and that I aim to do."

"Says it for me too," old Mose Cruikshank said stolidly, rolling his tobacco cud in his whiskered jaw.

"Me also," said Eduardo Chavez in his soft liquid way. "Maybe, like you say, boss, this is legal thing. Still it is wrong."

"You won't fight your people, is that it?"

"No," Chavez said, just as softly, "that is not it. If you don't see it, senor, talk will not help."

"All right," Lambeth said coldly. "You can pick up your wages. I'll stand behind any man who works for me, but I expect as much in return. Any more slackers and malcontents can speak up now."

Fats McEachin piped, "That's me," and Link Bardine and Red Hollister looked at each other and afterward at Lambeth, and both nodded. John's angry gaze shuttled on to Velez and Simon Jack. Velez shrugged, "I will stick," and Simon Jack grunted.

"Come to the office and I'll pay you off," Lambeth said curtly. "Pima, saddle my horse and Mrs. Lambeth's. Charley, you and the other fellows head out and I'll catch up."

Starr nodded, and went through the corral gate as the Pima opened it. John crossed to the house, followed by the six defecting hands, and entered his office. He calculated their wages to a day, signed the six identical checks, and stood in the doorway, watching them head for the corral to catch and ready their horses.

In spite of his stiff speech, Lambeth felt a vague unease for which he couldn't account at their departure. It was as if a last solid link with the old Nugget had been cut for good. . . .

His troubled thoughts cast back over the events of the past few days, and touched at once on Brazos Kane, on the rude revelation of the man's true character. It was still hard to believe, even after subsequent happenings pointed to the bitter truth. Kane had tried to kill him by a trick, then had cold-bloodedly shot down Pinto.

Yet at the first he had liked Kane. He was a rough, taciturn sort, the kind of man who had pioneered this country. Lambeth had found that such men, secure in their iron-hard independence, were a unique breed in all of human history; they leaned on nothing under the sun. You could pick them out in an instant from the others, the human flotsam which on an unpoliced frontier had reverted to the savagery of pre-tribal times. These hard kernels amid the dross possessed an integrity not absorbed or learned, and afterward hardship and self-sufficiency merely tempered it as fine as steel. Brazos Kane had impressed Lambeth as a particularly strong example of the breed; he was still non-plussed, even glum, at being so utterly wrong about a man.

It had shaken him, but not as much as learning of the brand-changing two days later. He had insisted, against Lila Mae' objection, on bringing in the sheriff and riding to Montalvo to confront O'Brien with the accusation and the evidence. She, backed by Charley Starr, had tried to convince him not to waste time, but to make fighting preparations at once. Still he had been enough primed with reckless anger to order Charley to accompany him, Charley's presence being his warning that he had taken all he intended taking from O'Brien. It had been a foolhardy thing, he now realized; if tempers had flared at Montalvo, he and his handful of men would have died on the spot.

Riding home in a mood of embattled anger, he had asked Charley Starr about those men he knew in Soledad; how soon could he have them here? Starr said it would take him at least a day to round them up; if he started now, he should return by midnight the next day.

Velez had begun a soft objection, and John had shot him a swift, impatient glance. "I'm sorry, Ramon; it's nothing against you. It's become obvious that I need a crew of trouble-shooters—and a foreman who can handle them. I'm sorry." Velez, his face like a seamed mask, had inclined his white head slightly, stiffly—that was all. Still the memory troubled Lambeth. Velez was no longer young, yet his competence was unquestioned.

Trying to justify his treatment of the foreman, Lambeth let his thoughts harden on what happened later. He had sat up late that night over the ranch tally books, and the next morning he rode out with the crew. By late afternoon, he came storming in to tell Lila Mae that the range count was decidedly low. "Wouldn't there be carcasses from a high winterkill?" he'd demanded. "That damned Velez tried to tell me that the blizzards must have drifted a lot of basin stock south through the passes. They were drifted, all right—it's as I suspected. Why should a big outfit like Montalvo trifle with a few stolen head? Obviously, it's part of a larger effort by O'Brien to break us slowly by bleeding us dry."

Lila Mae had watched him with wide, anxious eyes. "What do you think we'd ought to do, honey?"

"Only one thing. Let him know there's a limit to his greed and my patience. Move our stock onto the high summer grass Montalvo has always hogged to itself. And then, by God, let him try to stop us."

Late that evening they'd had a visitor—Liam Keogh. Lambeth had greeted the lawman coldly, intending not to be swayed by any placating words of Keogh's. He'd told them that Mike O'Brien had been given a two-day sentence in jail with no alternative of a fine. Judge Richie considered even this slight severity a dangerous legal precedent where a citizen's rights were concerned, considering the threadbare nature of the charge; he had stretched that point only because he understood the gravity of the situation and the danger of what O'Brien might do in his present frame of mind.

But Keogh's deep concern had been what would happen when O'Brien was released. "Mostly that depends on you," he had told John soberly. "I'm hoping that by day after tomorrow Mike'll be cooled off enough to stay cool, unless you crowd him. Then it won't take much."

"I could prefer charges for the cattle he stole from me," Lambeth had observed stonily. "That should extend his isolation somewhat. Say for five years or so."

Keogh had hauled a shaky breath, plainly reaching for patience. "Listen. If you do, nothing under the sun will hold his vaqueros back. And I damn well know Mike O'Brien isn't your guilty party. Today I covered every outfit in the basin, asking around, and I went over the ground with Simon Jack. All right. So far nothing, but I'm staying with it till I turn up the real story. And mister, you're going to wait on that, you hear?"

To that John had been coldly silent, and shortly Keogh took his leave, with an air of baffled and harried anger. It would be nothing to his reaction when he learned of their next move, and his hands would be solidly tied by the common-right law of public domain.

They had waited up for Charley Starr's return, and he arrived soon after midnight, red-eyed and exhausted, with six men in tow. They were a hardbitten crew, veteran "warriors," or mercenary troubleshooters. Probably their spotty backtrails ran six to the half-dozen, but in the mood still gripping him, Lambeth hadn't given a damn.

The drive onto the high grass had begun yesterday, John riding out with the crew again. They had driven several large bunches of their driftstock onto the supper range, while Montalvo riders looked on from a distance. Apparently O'Brien's daughter had given them orders not to interfere. Lambeth had seen her side with Keogh against her father, and evidently she realized that Montalvo could not continue to hog a common right. O'Brien would be in jail a good two days more, and by then they would have a good-sized herd on the high grass and be ready to hold them there against any countermeasures he took. Charley Starr had a couple of contacts in Soledad rounding up more warriors who should arrive tomorrow, and afterward the devil himself wouldn't move them off. . . .

The departing hands were riding out in a body, and now Lambeth left the house, heading for the corral where the Pima had left his saddled horse tied. He stepped into the saddle and rode out, angling northeast across the valley, lifting his horse into a slow lope to overtake Lila Mae and the crew, while a hint of bitter uncertainty continued to nag at him.

Am I wrong? he wondered; he had been angry, but with the full enormity of the move he had undertaken bearing home, the edge of his first heat was ebbing to cold concern. *It is a damnfool thing,* he thought. *O'Brien and I squabbling over a few acres of grass neither of us truly needs—what does it prove? And who really gains if men have to die, as it is a near-certainty they will?*

A wry, slow smile touched the Easterner's lips. He had always been a bit childish about the matter of taking life—his father, an inveterate sportsman, had placed a heavy rifle in his hands as soon as he was big enough to handle its firepower. He had been too young and impressionable for killing sport, and he remembered well the horror and revulsion he had felt when he had first killed a pheasant. For years he had choked down the feeling so as not to shame his father; he had grown accustomed to the man's world into which he was exclusively thrust—but never to the killing.

The way a man forced himself to overcome all manner of self-doubts and unbecoming weakness was a way of life that John Lambeth had learned of painful necessity, a way simple and stark and essential in a world of men. It could be summed up in one word: honor.

If you lived by honor, you could never shame a stern and demanding father. You could never let a man insult your wife and not pay in blood. And past a reasonable point, you could not accept the bullyragging and persecutions of an arrogant loudmouth like O'Brien. The Montalvo owner had crowded him beyond that point when he'd stolen the cattle.

Only Lila Mae, bedeviling him with her strange behavior, had ever put a crack in his manhood, but that time was done; now it was good between them, and John Lambeth was determined to keep it that way. *Above all,* he thought, *I must not let her see my doubts.*

And that, he knew, was the sum of his answer to those

same doubts. It was foolish yes, and he was wrong, but in the way all men were wrong, attaching a magical significance to words and customs encrusted with the hoary traditions of masculinity. A man was born into a world he had not made, and he had to live with it on its terms to live at all; and no matter that he recognized its pompous follies, its patent idiocies; he was as irrevocably bound by them as all men were, knowing or unknowing. . . .

His mood of gray musing broke as he sighted Lila Mae riding a little ahead of the crew. He passed them at a brisk clip and joined her. Since there was no immediate danger, he had assented to her riding out with him to watch the herd-move.

As they quartered onto the first broken hills of the northeast basin, the crew split off, led by Charley, toward the dusty flats below the high grass, where they had drifted much of the Nugget stock. Lambeth swung his arm toward a loaf-shaped ridge. "We can watch from up there, my dear. Quite safe, and I can recommend the view."

"Race you," she said, and quirted her sorrel toward the ridge. She came onto its crest and dropped from her saddle, breathless and laughing. Lambeth rode up in a moment, stepped down and threw her reins, then took her in his arms. She turned her back to his chest, tilting her face back laughing. "Goodness, my hair must be a sight."

"Then," he whispered, "I can't be accused of mussing it—can I?"

"Oh—honey, honey." After a moment she gently broke his hold and stepped away. "My, it's a fine view."

"Yes." He stood beside her, and in silence they watched the vast grass flats to the east, where a churning veil of dust rose above milling cattle as the crew hoorawed a jag of about a hundred head up a long shallow draw. And Lambeth said finally: "Well, there'll be no trouble today, at least. Think I'll ride down and join the boys. If you don't mind?"

"Sakes, no. I'll watch from here a spell."

"And you'll go directly home, then? I'd as soon you didn't go riding about the country alone just now."

She gave a little smile of assurance. As he dropped his arm from her waist, she twisted against him, her face lifted, saying with a fierce softness, "Honey, I'm so proud of you." She gave him his fill of her lips this time, and he felt their drug siphoning away his doubts, till all the world resided in her moist soft mouth. Dimly, he heard her whisper—"Keep me proud of you, John"—and then she broke it off with a nip of her small sharp teeth, and pulled back laughing.

With a sheepish grin, he mounted his horse and jogged off down the slope. It was worth it, he thought with a kind of dazed exultance. All the damned silly honor, the childish heroics, even the chance of death—all worth it because she made it so.

Lila Mae watched him go, a faint, speculative smile on her lips. He sat his saddle erectly despite the discomfort of his arm; there was a brisk and clear-eyed steadiness about him now, and the color in his face did not come from whiskey. *He's really braced up and taken hold*, she mused. *All from a little loving, a little getting mad too. Just see he stays so, and this fight is won.*

Strange, considering that only a few days ago she had been assuring Charley that John would have to go, and had even contrived a situation where Brazos Kane would have done the job for them. Yet in the last few days, she had been surprised by the resources that her wifely affections and the challenge of O'Brien's believed thievery had wakened in him. He had quit drinking; he had taken a tough and uncompromising hold on the situation she and Charley had created. So that now her thought, *why not keep it this way*, was no sudden one.

John was a gentleman, which Charley Starr was only in the past tense. He had more than the wealth she could inherit; he had fine family connections and influence in high places. All that could be useful. She had found herself getting pleasantly accustomed to his well-spoken dignity, his small attentions to her. More important, in finding the way to handle him, she could be sure of her power over him. Charley, with his rough cynicism and the instincts of his good upbringing thoroughly blunted, was also a slippery fish to handle.

Give John a little loving, keep him mad, and by all means let him enjoy every sop of rationalization he could offer his conscience. O'Brien would fight, and to a finish, but the finish would be his. Montalvo, broken and defeated, would be an example to all the small remaining outfits, which could be crowded into selling out. She did not even waste thought on building Nugget to any less than all of what Montalvo had always half-been, the whole power in Two Troughs Basin. *Why yes, someone will surely have to go, but why should it be John? You'll need Charley a while longer, but cross that bridge when you come to it.*

She smiled a little, thinking of the jealous wrath she knew was coming to a head in Charley. Before this she had placated Charley by tried and trusted means, and she could again. Charley was a man, and men, like fishes, could apply only so many variations of struggle once they were hooked, while a shrewd angler could head off each one. Lila Mae hummed contentedly to herself; things were going very well. . . . That six of the eight original hands had quit in a body, she counted to the good; their places would be filled by more of Charley's friends when they arrived.

She watched the drive a while longer, then gathered her skirt in one hand, stepped into her saddle, and swung the sorrel toward home. The excitement in her held strongly, causing her to use her quirt and small blunt spurs cruelly. As she neared the ranch buildings, the animal was blowing and lathered.

Then, coming around the tack barn, she felt a thin shock. Charley was leaning against the building, his arms folded. He said quietly, "Get down."

She reined in the prancing sorrel, her voice coming shrill with anger. "You fool! Why aren't you with—"

"Get down," Charley repeated, now with an ominous softness. She let her eyes narrow, studying him carefully. Behind his set expression, she saw a raw and jealous violence held in thin check, and it was no time for rough words. She was in no mood to soften him, but she bit back a sharp word and slowly dismounted then, facing him. "Maybe you'd better make some sense of this, mister."

"I cut back right after we left you. Don't worry, I'll have a handy-sounding excuse for Lambeth. Maybe."

"Now what would you mean by 'maybe'?"

"I mean, puss, I came back here to wait for you. We need a talk about things. Maybe I don't like some of what I've seen, and maybe I'll have something else to tell your precious dude."

"Don't be a jealous fool." Lila Mae kept her voice even with an effort. "Do I have to explain my reason all over?"

"You're playing it pretty hot and heavy," Starr said gently. "Enough so I judge you've picked yourself another reason, one I'd expect you to deny."

"That's nonsense. Though, supposing you're not inclined to believe me, I wouldn't try that threat again. He'd never take anyone's word against mine."

It was a sheathed threat of her own, and it drew a wicked smile from Charley. "That's bluff, or plain dumb of you. If a man insults the poor fool's wife, what'll he do? Do I have to draw a map of what'll happen to him if he crowds me as he did Kane?" He shook his head gently. "You bought your ticket with Charley for this ride, and you're going all the way with him, sweetheart, right to the end of the line. You do things your way, but don't ever try to shut me out."

The banked anger in her flared blindly, and she brought back her quirt to slash at his mocking smile. He grabbed her wrist, and she whipped her free palm across his cheek, backhanding him with a second blow before he captured that hand too. She caught her breath at the savage bite of his fingers in her flesh, and he shook her almost gently.

"You're going to think about that, puss. You don't stay mad long, and then you'll think. You've fetched your old dog Trey with a whistle so long that you've forgotten he has teeth. I wouldn't forget again. I'll be around when you need me, but bear in mind that I hold a nice sharp ax any time I want to drop it."

He let her go, and turned and stalked to where his horse waited. She stood unmoving, rubbing her arms, and watched him mount and swing out of the yard without a glance at her. Lila Mae picked up her reins and walked the sorrel to the corrals. As she tugged viciously at the cinch to loosen it, a cool voice at her back gave her an unpleasant start.

"I will walk him if you please, senora, and turn him in."

She smoothed her face to a careful mask and turned to face Delores Velez, standing stoutly with her arms akimbo. The woman's face was bovine and placid, and Lila Mae handed her the reins with a curt nod and stepped past her, heading for the house.

She worried her pouted underlip with her teeth, walking slowly. How much had the woman seen—or heard? *Damn her black eyes*, she thought, *prying greaser bitch*, and then deciding that it was of no account, dismissed Velez' wife from her thoughts. She had a few moments of bitter cud-chewing over Charley Starr, a more slippery fish than she had known. Then coming onto the veranda, she paused with a hand on the doorlatch, the little smile on her lips. One of Charley's Soledad friends he had imported might be less friendly toward him for the right amount of money, when the time came.

CHAPTER FOURTEEN

FOR BRAZOS in his lonely hideaway, the time dragged slowly. He slept most of the time; he drank a lot of water, smoked an endless chain of cigarettes, and ate when he was hungry, cooking a quota of his grub each night. The deep inroad he was making in his food supplies was a good augur of his comeback. His rawhide system would mend itself with rest and time, and he wasted no concern on that score.

Pepe had provided him with a crude crutch, a knife-worked sapling with its upper end crotched for a shoulder brace. With it he could manage an awkward hobble, but the shooting pain that grabbed his leg on the first attempt, leaving him dizzy and panting, inclined him to move about as little as possible, careful to put no weight on his hurt leg. The limit of his exertions carried him to the cave mouth to freshen his canteen from the tiny waterfall that chuckled down past the outer ledge. He spent his wakeful daylight hours on the ledge in the sun, dozing or reading. His present stock consisted of two thumb-tattered Hawthorne novels and a dilapidated copy of Tom Paine's *Common Sense,* and soon he knew them almost by heart. When the sleepless hours came at night, there was nothing to do but think.

Able to shift for himself with the fever past, he had told Pepe not to take the risk of returning to the cave; he'd taken enough long chances on Brazos' account. But Ramon Velez' failure to show up worried him; a good deal could have happened since he'd talked to Raquel, but he wondered why—unless he'd badly misjudged Velez or unless Raquel had failed to get him word—the Nugget foreman hadn't come. Velez or Raquel herself might have decided that the fate of one hurt and hunted mustanger did not outweigh the personal risk; that, along with a multitude of morose thoughts, was unanswerable speculation, and he settled down to a forced and chafing wait.

He thought often of the day Raquel had spent here—how quickly it had seemed to go—turning over her words, her movements and moods, and was mildly amazed, since they had turned every subject into a war of words, that memory framed as many pleasant details of her. He was too unused to women was the trouble; particularly one like her, but maybe it was as Pop Melaven used to say: "Only thing you need to know about a woman, they ain't one worth a damn unless they's some spice with the sugar." Brazos grinned with the thought, having a notion of his own, which was that none of it was worth anything without the gentleness, and that he had seen for himself.

On his sixth day in the cave, he tried out his makeshift crutch, finding that his bad leg was able to accommodate a gingerly weight. He did some practice hobbling around the cave, then not wanting to overdo it but restless with waiting, stripped down, soaped and bathed himself, and donned the change of clothes Raquel had left with him. It was a country where a man was used to bathing when he had the rare chance, but sick as he'd been, he had been getting genuinely rank and the change brought a keen lift to his spirits.

He was more used to his beard, and scowled for a wary time at the shaving gear she'd left, but in fact finally heated some water. He took the opportunity to burn his filth-encrusted clothes, then painstakingly whittled away the stiff scrub of his beard. He felt even better, almost a different man, as afterward he sunned himself on the ledge in the cave mouth, sometimes rubbing his palm over his tender jaw.

Well after midday an alien noise tickled him out of a light doze, bringing him half-erect, and then he caught it again, the ring of iron on rock. He felt his holstered gun in the rolled shellbelt at his side, drew the weapon and cocked it muffled against his sleeve, not taking his eyes off the downcanyon bend. As the rider reached the bend he saw it was Raquel, and he lowered his gun and inched to his feet, and waited for her to ascend to the ledge.

He extended his hand and swung her onto it; he had a sharp word ready, but seeing the haggard strain that marked her face and sobered her dark eyes, he softened it. "Reckoned you wouldn't come again."

"I thought you might need more grub." She moved into the cave and laid down a bulging floursack she carried. She avoided his eyes, and he had the feeling she was covering her thoughts. "I was careful that I wasn't followed."

"That's all right. Only Velez never came."

"I know. Bernardo has not had the chance to see him, so he said; he will try again today." She rubbed a palm over her cheek, a vague and tired gesture. "A lot has happened. I—"

110

"Sit down and tell it."

He learned then of the brand-altered steers, and of what had followed at Montalvo. And of John Lambeth's importing of toughs, his moving Nugget cattle on the high range. Brazos broke in with a flat disbelief, "Your pa is standing still for that?"

"He will surely not, when he comes home from the calaboose tomorrow. But already Nugget is dug in solidly on the high grass and they will fight to hold it."

Brazos said slowly, "Then you've been holding the lid down alone," now understanding her worn and harried look.

She nodded bitterly. "And every day it grows harder. They see Nugget throwing more and more cattle onto the high grass, while I tell them to have patience. They listen—but it is only deaf respect paid to the mayordomo's daughter, do you see? They are only waiting for my father to come home and lead them in the fight."

"Fools," Brazos said quietly.

Her head came up swiftly; he saw the dark flash of her eyes. "Fools? What do you know, Anglo? I am a fool too, if to be one of them and understand their anger makes me a fool. Do you think Montalvo is only boundary lines marked by a gringo surveyor? This was their mother country before you swallowed it, and they know what you Anglos consider them: less than dogs. In holding all of the old Montalvo intact, including what you call public domain, its people have found their great strength and pride; they have forced the Anglos' respect for them as more than another crowd of greasers—a Montalvo man takes the feeling with his mother's milk, it goes so far back."

The fire and passion of her held Brazos mute, but then he said stubbornly, "We talked enough last time so I know the books you've read, the ideas you've brushed against. There's a bigger law than your tradition or the Anglo government's ruling. It's a law called change—evolution—with nothing expected from it. The Anglos are the power, and unless your Montalvo people see the way of change, there'll soon be no Montalvo."

Her shoulders lifted slightly and fell in a sigh. "I know. By holding them back I'm fighting for what they would fight for. Theirs is a wrong way—but how to make them see it?"

They were sitting on the floor of the cave, Brazos with his bad leg outstretched to ease it. Raquel sat tailor-fashion with her legs crossed, her arms folded beneath her breasts, drawing the faded yellow waist taut across them. They formed two firm half-globes and were fuller than he had thought—a womanly fullness. He lowered his eyes, feeling the slow heat in his neck. Damn—a man's mind seemed drawn to such details. She spoke, so softly that he glanced up: "What?"

"I said, I am sorry I was sharp with you, arguing so, when I was here before."

"I wondered some about it."

"I suppose I was sharp for the same reason I am here to-day. I . . ." He felt the reluctance in her hesitance, but she was too forthright not to finish what she had begun, and she said: "I suppose I feel drawn to you, and I must fight it. Have you ever fought something that way—trying to hate it because you know it's not good for you? Do you see?"

"Maybe."

"I don't want to like you," she said vehemently. "It is wrong—not because you are poor or a drifting man or an Anglo. Because there is nothing in you but a need for revenge. That is wrong—and you are wrong."

"You could be wrong too."

"What do you mean?"

"A man's like anything else. He changes as time goes on. It can be for the better."

"And have you changed that way?"

Brazos did not answer. He brooded at the ground, rubbing one hand gently, absently, along his game leg, feeling the mild itch in his healing wound. What concern was any of it to him? The answer came almost at once, and it was oddly welcome. He was beholden to Raquel, to Velez and Pepe, and this Two Troughs country was their home. Their roots were planted here, deep and sure, touching their lives with meaning. Himself rootless, he had to grope for the significance of this, and though vaguely enough, it was coming to him; he was beginning to understand the full meaning of the anger and contempt she had shown him. Because she prized deeply the meaning in her life, she understood clearly that its lack was a disease which, if it did not kill a man young, would turn his sound parts one by one into scar tissue, leaving a living husk. He had lived half his life with a man like that.

And he had met another man, Pepe Garcia, who probably could not read or write his name but yet who knew how to crowd all the meaning of a man's life into a ramshackle one-room hovel. Life had kicked that peppery little man into a corner too, but he had it thrown and hogtied all the same. How many times could a man turn his back and ride away from what troubled him until, inevitably, it ceased to touch

112

him? Yet the simple goodness that filled Pepe Garcia's life could be shattered by the same explosion of violence that would affect every life in this basin if it came. *But not you,* Brazos mused. *You can always turn your back and ride away from it, can't you?*

He was silent for so long that Raquel said finally, softly, "It was a mistake to come here. Now I'll go," and rose to her feet.

Brazos stood too, awkwardly crutch-braced by one hand, and he could not think what to say. Then he felt her eyes again, dark and intense, and she said suddenly, "Why did you shave?"

"Your idea. I don't know how to—"

"You have a good mouth and chin." The dark strain had left her eyes. "I didn't think . . . but it was your eyes. They were ugly, and I thought your face would be. It is not, and your eyes are not now . . ." Her voice was trailing softly, and she raised her hand till it touched his arm, and let it slip upward to his shoulder. "They are different," she whispered, and the breath lifted into his throat and caught hard; his hand was almost rough pulling her in, his mouth coming into her tilted lips. Her mouth broke moistly, and her warm young passion swelled into him with the fierce sudden molding of her whole body. Her fingers worked on his neck and back, till it ended in the need for breath and he could say huskily, "This is a damnfool thing—"

"Don't say that!" Her eyes went stormy with a near anger. "Don't ever say that again. . . ."

It was much later and shortly after dark that they caught the first sound of a slow-coming rider from downcanyon. They had hardly noticed when darkness came, except to build a fire, and now they started and met each others' eyes almost guiltily.

"Maybe it's Ramon," she whispered. "He could probably only get away after dark."

"Wait," Brazos murmured, drawing his gun. They waited tensely till he caught a low halloo from the canyon floor. It was Velez, and Brazos called back. After a heavy, shuffling ascent, Velez stepped stolidly into the firelight. He gave Raquel a surprised, appraising look, but made no comment beyond a polite greeting. He squatted on his heels and spread his calloused palms to the warmth of the compact blaze, and told them that he had gotten Raquel's message from Bernardo only this afternoon. Tonight he had told Starr he was riding to town to visit his sister Luz and her family, to which Starr had grunted a narrow-eyed assent. After leaving Nugget, he had waited on the road awhile in case Starr should send a man into Diablo to check on him. "If I heard one come, I would have gone fast to Luz's. Only after, I came on here. This canyon and this cave, I could find blindfold."

"All the old hands sloped?" Brazos asked.

"The lot, except me and the Pima. It pleases Starr that I stay on, so that he can ride my tail as I rode his. But the law has been keeping Simon Jack busy."

Brazos nodded. "Lucky for me, if he threw Keogh off like I figure."

"He did, but there is now the matter of these stolen steers. The sheriff and Simon Jack went over the floor of Blanco Canyon, but all the Pima turns up is the ashes of a branding fire and buried close by a running iron wrapped in a gunny sack. This tells nothing. But Starr and Sholto went late into Diablo the night before these cows are found, for a few drinks they say. They came in very late, acting very drunk, but maybe not. Maybe that is when the work is done, eh? That day I'd had Mose Cruikshank working with Sholto to watch him, and the two of them were to finish popping the brush deep in Blanco Canyon the next day. Sholto knew this, and it was the next day he and Mose find the cattle there. They must have been waiting to set up something like this.

"Meantime our senor moves the Nugget cows onto the high grass while the Montalvo vaqueros watch and so far only wait. It was up there today that I met my cousin, who told me Raquel is doing her best to head off trouble." Velez sent the girl an oblique look. "Bernardo and the others have much bitterness about this, that you hold them back while your papa is not there to say otherwise."

"I know their feeling, Ramon. When Mike returns, then it will break, and what can the sheriff do alone?"

Brazos said, "He could send for the territorial marshal, the army. Squabble's over federal-declared public domain, isn't it?"

"Si, but both sides have their rights there," Velez observed. "And when do the government people move to stop a bad thing before it starts? In Lincoln County, when Chisum and McSween started a blood bath, wasn't it so? Ha! You Yanquis, Brazos, are ver' jealous of your right to spit in anyone's eye. Let the army fight the redskins, you all say, and let us fight our own."

Brazos stared reflectively at the fire for a long time, finally provoking Velez to a curious question. "Just pitching pennies," Brazos said. "Now I'll pitch you one. As I read it, the key men are Lambeth and O'Brien. Get 'em to pull in their horns and your big trouble's stopped cold."

"Ha," Velez said harshly. "Listen, my friend. You have not seen our senor lately. He stopped the drinking, which seemed good, but what came with it was not. Even before the business of the changed brands, he began to interfere with me, to ride the crew with wrongheaded orders. Delores, who keeps her big ears cocked always to the wind, says his senora has built him up with talk. He had a big head the morning we rode into Montalvo, and he handled the matter badly. That Senor Mike would blow up was only to be expected. Now, when our senor talks, it is her words that come out. He would hear nothing of her that is bad. Before, when Ramon Velez talked, he listened. Now—I can only stay on. A place is in a man's blood, and I am too old for new starts. But I tell you, it is a hard thing to take."

Brazos lowered his eyes. This was Velez' great pride, his foremanship of an Anglo outfit and the respect that went with it—hard-won by a man of his race—a pride raw and defaced by John Lambeth's bad judgment.

"As for cooling off Senor Mike," Velez added dourly, "I would as soon try to muzzle *el tigre*. Montalvo alone has always held the high grass, and he is not the man to give an inch."

Brazos rubbed his chin thoughtfully. "Still, we know what's going on that they don't. We don't know all the wherefores, but we know the who."

"Yes, that is pretty sure. Mrs. Lambeth from the first has wanted Charley to be foreman, and my wife, who does not miss much, has seen Starr and her together with eyes for each other." Velez puckered his snowy brows. "Today, she saw something else. The boss and Mrs. Lambeth rode out with our crew this morning to watch us drive the cattle. They split off and left us, and then Charley Starr says he must ride back to headquarters for something. A little later, Senor Lambeth joined us, as he has been doing of late, and it was a good hour before Starr returned. He told the senor that his cinch strap was frayed and he returned to get a different saddle. He did change his saddle, Delores said, but then he went to wait by the tack barn. When the senora rode in, they spoke together— and the words were bitter, for she tried to hit Starr with her quirt."

Brazos carefully shifted his leg against another twinging cramp. "Look. If Starr came to Nugget on her account, and

115

he must have, it means they knew each other from before."

"Ah," Velez said softly.

"That could mean there's some dirty linen hung on the back trail that could be traced if a man took a mind. If I put a bug in Keogh's ear and he figured it was worth following up, he might find something that would pull the roof down on 'em."

"But you daren't go to the sheriff," Raquel said. "And if you did, he would probably laugh at such a story."

"If he did not," Velez growled, "it would take much time we don't have to do the digging back."

Brazos hardly heard them, already feeling the glimmer of an idea on the heels of his own words. *Now that's a notion. They set up the lie for you—Starr and Lila. Play it out all the way, and you might trap them in it.*

He talked for a long time, slowly because he was unsorting the details of his plan even as he told it. And he said finally: "That's about it. With Raquel's help, we can convince her pa it's worth a try. But with Lambeth—the whole thing is, we'll have to crack him wide open."

Velez gave a grave slow nod. "Yes, that is the way. A hard thing to do to a man, but that is the way surely."

CHAPTER FIFTEEN

THERE HAD BEEN RAIN early last night, and its afterscent clung with a clean coolness to the morning air. Liam Keogh sniffed it without much pleasure as he left his boarding house. He had unthinkingly put down a heavy breakfast on a worried stomach, and his dourness deepened as he hit the street. The spring rains had made it a shallow channel, chopped by traffic to a stocky mire which balled up the soles of his boots before he'd gone ten steps. Swearing mildly under his breath, the sheriff slogged toward his office, head bent as he nursed his cold pipe.

He had put in a good deal of legwork over the last two days, trying to turn up the identity of the brand-changers. After questioning all the Montalvo people down to the small children, he had gone to every rancher, farmer and squatter in the Two Troughs basin. He'd kept a suspicious eye on Simon Jack Pima as the two of them prowled old trail deep into the hills; he still had the feeling that the Pima deliberately dogged his job when he'd had him tracking Brazos Kane. But this time, knowing what was at stake, Simon Jack had kept his nose to the trail like a restless hound. The trouble was, you might as well trail a bird across some stretches of this north basin, especially the Blanco Canyon area. Keogh was sure of Mike O'Brien's innocence, and while some other Montalvo individual might be the guilty party, he knew the ones who shared Montalvo patronage to a man. Strong in their pride, with not a petty thief among them. *Hell, no matter who it was, all he has to do is deny it.*

Keogh achieved the rickety porch fronting his office and paused to knock his boots clean. John Lambeth was past argument, and Mike would be, on learning that Nugget had moved onto his summer range. Since he had to release O'Brien today, it would be best to tell him now and try to argue him out of a rash countermove. Nearly twenty years ago Keogh and O'Brien had shared a jail cell in Soledad for a drunken hoorawing of the town, and as he'd known it would, a spell in jail had now cooled Mike down. *But that won't help with something fresh to start his temper off. We're neither of us cubs any more, but some ways a man don't change...*

Bleakly he dug out his key, then frowned at finding the office door unlocked. Ralph Means, his deputy, jailor and nightman, had been warned often enough to keep the place locked at night. Ralph was slow-witted, but he could follow an order. Stepping inside, he found the office deserted and Ralph's cot in the corner unmussed. He said sharply, "Ralph?"

There were scuffling sounds from the cellblock, and a man's voice oddly muffled. Keogh lifted the key ring off its hook, unlocked the door and went through to the far cell. It had been occupied by Mike O'Brien, but now it held only Ralph Means, feebly beating his heels against the wall. He was trussed hand and foot on the cot, and gagged by a dirty towel.

Keogh got the gag off, struggled with the tight knots, and swearing, took out his pocketknife. "I ought to cut your throat with it. What happened?"

"They was that girl of O'Brien's and one of their Mexes," Ralph husked, his mild eyes watering. "Hell, Li, I didn't think nothing of it when she come knocking, though it was 'round midnight. Said she needed to tell her pa something, and you told me she was on your side in all this here."

"And it never entered your—" Keogh barked, then checked himself and said resignedly, "Go on. You let them in."

"Yes'r. Had my gun ready, but I put it away then. Right off this Mex yanks out a gun and shoves it in my side. 'Por favor,' he says, 'I must trouble you for the keys.'" Ralph scratched his tow thatch as he eased stiffly to his feet. "Uh, he was a short 'un, kind of, and stocky, and he favored one leg. Had a sort of crutch."

"Hell, man, you must have seen his face."

"Nos'r. He had a big sombrero, and a poncho tucked high around his chin. So the girl lets out her pa, and he made me lay down here and cinched me up."

"Get over to the stable and get my horse ready. Yours too."

Ralph left at a hobbling run. Keogh took a rifle from the gunrack, scooped a fistful of loose shells out of a desk drawer and began to load it, his mind full of angry questions. O'Brien had no stove-up crewman that he knew of, and why should the girl break him out on the eve of his legal release? For once he was damned well going to get some answers. He heard a rider dismount outside, and then Simon Jack appeared in the doorway. "You wantem Pima for trail today, boss?"

"You'd have a hell of a time missing this one," Keogh said flatly. "Come on!"

The sheriff's baffled anger became complete bewilderment before they had covered a quarter-mile. At the edge of town Simon Jack had picked up the tracks of three horses with absurd ease, and from there the sign clung plainly to the soaked dirt of the East Pass road, until it forked north on a side trail. No effort had been made to cover the sign, and no effort had been spared to hold it to bitter travel.

As the country roughened, the trail straggled over some ridges, wound aimlessly around others, and made its way with infuriating deliberation through canyons whose clogging of wet brush filled them with steaming heat under the mounting sun. Keogh cursed and sweated doggedly for a full hour, and when he was about to turn back and head for Montalvo headquarters, Simon Jack pulled up his horse and pointed.

"There."

Keogh saw a pale stem of smoke lift above a timbered ridge, and he knew that a small open park lay beyond it. "You and me will ride in," he told the Pima. "Ralph, you hold off five minutes and follow us. This time keep your gun out."

Ralph grunted a sheepish assent, and Keogh let Simon Jack lead off up the ridgetop, and they descended the opposite side. Keogh took the lead as they rode out of the thinning timber, and then he pulled up swearing under his breath.

Brazos Kane sat on a folded tarp by the fire, one leg outstretched, its thigh bulky with bandages. O'Brien was squatted beside him, and they were drinking from tin cups and talking quietly. Raquel was feeding the fire with small sticks, and Pepe Garcia hunkered beside it, making a fourth. Pepe reached a rag-wrapped fist and lifted a bubbling coffeepot from the fire and filled a cup. Nobody bothered to glance at Keogh, and he warily nudged his mount into motion and pushed into the camp.

Pepe Garcia glanced up then, a polite smile on his ugly face. "Ah. If you will light down, senor the sheriff, your coffee is ready." Keogh looked at Pepe's broad sombrero and poncho and thought mechanically, *There's your Mexican. No, by God —the limp. It was Brazos Kane.*

In utter bewilderment now, he dismounted and dropped his reins. Simon Jack, already on the ground, picked them up and led both horses over three other ground-tied animals. Keogh felt foolish standing with the half-pointed gun in his hand, and more so because none of them were armed. Two rifles and a pistol were stacked in plain sight on a flat rock well off from the fire.

"What the hell," he got out, "is this? Mike, what're you doing here?"

Mike drained his cup before lifting a languid glance. This was, Keogh wrathfully knew, the kind of practical joke that O'Brien reveled in. His eyes were very gray and sparkling in his broad sober face. "Enjoying good coffee and better talk. Ye'll join us, Liam."

"I'll—" Keogh choked, and bit down on his tongue for a careful five seconds. He slapped his gun into its holster, dropped on his haunches by the fire, thumbed back his hat, and pointed the thumb at Mike. "There's something behind all this, and I'll give you one minute to make it clear."

"Drink your coffee, Liam. You always was an astute lad." He nudged Brazos. "Didn't I tell you he was astute? Now, Liam, if Mr. Kane had rode in alone and told you that John Lambeth's pretty fluff of a wife and his new foreman Starr had contrived to frame me up, what would you say, eh?"

Keogh eyed him ominously. "Without solid proof, you know what I'd say."

"So would I," O'Brien said agreeably. "And what would you say if he further told you this same fluff and Starr had fixed it for Kane to kill Lambeth and Pinto DeVries to kill Kane? I'm talking of their misfired plan which has you on Mr. Kane's trail."

"I'd throw him in jail," Keogh snapped, his patience fraying out. "Listen, Mike—"

"I'd do the same." A deep chuckle broke in O'Brien's throat. "Ah, but the cunning way he set this up, breaking a man about to be freed from jail! Now what could that man do but listen?"

Keogh said flatly, "I'd say he's fed you some taffy you swallowed whole," and shuttled his angry stare to Brazos who was idly swirling the dregs in his cup.

"He don't say much," O'Brien grinned, "and for a fact I only heard him out because my girl insisted. But it made sense enough, and he's willing to back his word with action. I'll take a chance on that, and I'd advise you do the same, Liam. Go on, lad, tell him."

As Brazos talked quietly and slowly, Ralph Means drifted in, dismounted and stood scratching his head, then accepted the cup of coffee handed him by a beaming Pepe. At first Keogh listened out of angry curiosity, breaking in roughly with sharp questions. Brazos answered him patiently, and

Keogh found himself studying the man as carefully as his words. Kane's face had a clean pleasant boyishness, and the look of hard insolence that had concentrated in his eyes seemed eased away. Keogh realized that some of it was the effect of his shaving off his beard, yet he thought with a sudden conviction, *Hell, he ain't much more than a boy. Times he's known have marked him all right, but not the way Lambeth's wife told it.* As Mike had said, the story made sense, and it explained a number of things that made little sense by themselves.

When Brazos paused, his faint, tired and friendly smile erased even the toughness. "Figured if I just gave myself up and told you all that, you'd think I was running a sandy. You might be disposed to listen if I convinced Mr. O'Brien first and then tolled you way out here to lay it out for you with him siding me."

Keogh grimaced, rubbing his sore hip. "You could have outsmarted yourself, boy. It's a judge and jury that'll need the convincing. But you say you got a way of proving your story out, so let's hear it."

"It's a gamble, sheriff. Maybe a long one. But if it works, it'll stop your war that's brewing too. I put it to Mr. O'Brien, and he agrees it's worth a try."

"I needn't tell you," Mike put in, "how I take this move by Lambeth onto my grass, public domain be damned. That the man's a simple goat for others don't change the fact. Kane figures he can be showed, and I'm willing to wait. Just so long, ye mind."

Brazos nodded. "Reason I needed to talk to you, sheriff. I'll want your help."

It was nearly noon when Brazos and the O'Briens returned to Montalvo. They had come directly here the night before after breaking out O'Brien, and by the time they had reached the headquarters the big Irishman was wholly game for the plan as Brazos had told it. He had assembled all his vaqueros in the yard by lantern-light and firmly pulled the teeth of the feisty ones by telling them any countermove by Montalvo would be held off till the idea was given a fair chance. And now with Keogh's assurance of help, there was nothing to do but wait for day's end before setting things in motion.

O'Brien's cheery mood held, as he whiled away the forenoon by showing Brazos around the place, proudly pointing out his blooded horses and a fenced pasture where he kept experimental breeders. "If a man's to grow with the times, he needs

121

to try new ways." He added with dry significance, "and to hold onto what's his. Give me a few years and Montalvo will need all the grass it can get. Let's go in; grub'll be on."

The dining room table was resplendent with snowy linen and fine silverware and a variety of steaming dishes, enough for a feast. Only three places were set, and Brazos had the uneasy feeling that O'Brien was trying deliberately to over-awe him. All this was a far cry from anything he had known, and even Raquel looked strange and different in a fine white dress that rustled with starch. She was directly across from him so that he had to fill his eyes with the startling contrast between her dress and light gray eyes and her olive-tinted skin and glistening hair. She looked older and more self-assured, the rightful mistress here, her manner one of cordial and careful warmth toward a guest. He found himself resenting that, also the way O'Brien kept sizing him to see how he was taking it all. Even the housekeeper, gliding in and out of the room, overseeing the meal with a noiseless efficiency, was a slow irritation. *Ease off. There's a mean time ahead and you're wound up for it and spooking yourself.*

Afterward he forced himself to relax over a fine liqueur and imported Havana while he listened to O'Brien's onrun of pleasant chatter. It was perhaps an hour later, still well ahead of time, when he made a show of consulting the battered old watch that was his one legacy from Pop Melaven. He excused himself, went out to the corral where a smiling stableboy in spotless white cottons insisted on readying his horse, and led the animal back to the outside gate of the walled patio adjoining the dining room. Its French doors were open, and Mike and Raquel were deep in conversation. Then she glanced outside, spoke quietly to her father, and came out across the patio to the gateway.

"Well," she smiled, but she swallowed quickly and he saw the dark worry in her eyes.

Brazos passed a slow glance around the courtyard. Its walls were fretted with the cracks of age and a tangle of rioting vines. The dark old salt cedars laid cool long shadows across the flagstones, and their dusky green seemed to simmer and drowse in the hot midday. The quiet peace of the ancient house and grounds was heightened somehow by the distant bark of a dog and the cries of playing children. A part of his mind reached out to it, the part jaded by hardship and cynicism and old trouble. The rest of him stood off, alien and unsure, and he brought his gaze back to the girl and saw her as one with this place, unable to separate them in his mind.

He cleared his throat gently. "A fine home. A fine life you have here, you and your father."

"Yes." Her eyes were grave and intent. "Yes?"

"Nothing. Only I wish . . . " He dropped his gaze to his hat and slowly turned the brim in his hands. "It's kind of late."

She shook her head with the quick anger he'd seen before, taking a step that brought her close to him. "Don't put a double meaning in your words. I am not a halfway woman, Brazos, and I have said all I feel. Will you make me say it again?"

"Hard not to take some things into account."

"So—only a child or a fool doesn't. I'm neither of those, nor a weak pale thing afraid of the sunlight. You are a reading man; you must have read this line—" She paused with a little frown . . ." 'Perhaps it seemed to me that I had several more lives to live—' "

"—'and could not spare any more time for that one.' Well, that's right, how I feel, only . . ."

"So do I. We will have a new life now, do you see?" There was a fierce gentleness in her hands, drawing his face down to her tilted one, and he tasted the soft storm suppressed in her, the fire and passion, and had no arguments left. It drugged him against everything but the hushed insistence of her words. "When you come back . . . when you come back, and oh, you must . . ."

It stayed with him as he rode away, heading northeast by the sun for Blanco Canyon—the drug of her words and body and lips. He shook it away, reaching for the cool head he would need. He quartered around and halted when he heard a rider coming, and wasn't surprised to see that it was O'Brien.

"I'll side you a ways," Mike said, and they put their horses apace. Mike took out a cheroot, clipped the end with a gold cutter and lighted it. He rolled it meditatively between his teeth and said around it, "We was talking after you quit the table. You can guess about what."

Brazos said nothing. Mike blew smoke and squinted at the blue sunny haze of it. "I was a ne'er-do-well soldier of fortune before coming to Montalvo, but maybe you've heard that. First time I saw her mother, I knew what I could work for and what I could become as a man. It took five years in the doing, and then we had one good year before . . . but it changed me. A man can change, even one who began as a copper-wheedling guttersnipe in the Dublin, and then Boston, slums."

Mike's light blue eyes swung on him with a merciless intensity. "I saw in you what I didn't like, when we first met. I'll concede that I didn't look far enough; still you're no fitter a man now for my girl than I was for her mother. You're my own kind, one I understand almost too well. Neither are ye a fool; if you find a reason to stop and take a reckoning of yourself, you'll have all the guts you need to shape yourself over. But you'll want a damned strong reason."

Brazos met his stare coldly. "I think it is."

Mike's lips quirked. "Won't knuckle to any man a damn inch, will you? We're alike right enough." He took the cheroot from his lips and flicked off ash. "Hell, if my girl is going to take a chance on you, I've no choice but to go along. She's made up her mind, and it's a day I knew had to come. Now, I'm thinking it'll be well if I bring up a party of my men to Nugget and hold them out of sight in case . . ."

"No. If you're spotted, it'll give the whole thing away. There's five of us to work it out. If we aren't enough, it won't matter."

"In that event you'd be putting your head in a nice tight noose for nothing. Though I'll admit it's largely what you're taking on your neck for all of us that inclines me kindly toward you." He reined up, his light glance slanting hard against Brazos'. "Man, you hold a precious thing in your hand. See you handle it gently."

He swung off back the way he had come, and Brazos watched him go, reflecting that Mike might have meant the touchy job ahead. And knowing damned well that he hadn't.

CHAPTER SIXTEEN

BRAZOS REACHED Blanco Canyon about two by the sun, and he plunged into it and held to its boulder-strewn floor for a half-mile. When he came to a place where the downtapering walls had broken in a slide of rubble, he dismounted and led the blue up to the rim. It was a rough climb, the free shale cascading away beneath his feet and crutch and the blue's iron shoes, and his rubbery leg gave out on the rimrock. He rested briefly, then ground-tied the blue in some scraggly firs back off the rim. He took his position, settling on his hips in the bare shadow of a boulder teetering on the slide edge.

The sun poured relentlessly onto the rocky terrain, every bare surface reflecting its oven-blast as the afternoon waned. Brazos stayed as he was, rifle and canteen at his side, occasionally shifting his leg against a dull steady ache, while his body in its soaked clothes itched with the sweat he could feel puddling in his boots. When, at last, he heard the sound of riders moving in from the canyon mouth, he picked up his rifle and levered in a cartridge. He waited, hugging the boulder, keeping a good view of the canyon floor.

The Pima came into sight first, and John Lambeth was close behind him. Brazos saw what Velez had meant; there was little of the easy-going dude left about Lambeth. His face in the shadow of his hatbrim was angry and out of patience, and the drift of his voice had a querulous harshness: "The devil! Not even a cow dropping along the way. Are you sure this was the canyon?"

Simon Jack grunted, "Sure, boss. Same place before. Pima think maybe cowstealing man drive more, same place. Lookem here, sun high, two-three hour ago. Plenty Nugget cow, all brands changed same. Little farther more, you see."

Brazos laid his sights along the glossy rump of Lambeth's sorrel, hesitating. This was a rough way, but it had to look good. Gently he squeezed off the shot. The clapping echoes racketed from wall to wall; the sorrel squealed and reared, careening in a wild circle. Lambeth, caught totally off guard, was jolted from his saddle. Brazos had chosen a rock-

125

free stretch to drop him, and Lambeth struck hard and rolled over twice. He lay on his face stunned as his horse bolted a short way and halted. Simon Jack dropped from his saddle as the Nugget owner pawed dazedly to his hands and knees, and helped him stand.

Brazos stood to, holding his crutch shoulder-braced and his Winchester loosely trained on Lambeth, who asked, "He got a handgun?"

Simon Jack looked up casually at the same time that he stepped away from Lambeth, who staggered and nearly fell. "No handgun. Rifle on horse."

Lambeth set his feet apart swaying. His jacket and face were smeared with dirt and his nose was bleeding. "What the devil," he muttered.

Brazos made an awkward descent of the slide, holding his bad leg utterly stiff. He didn't have to feign the effort it cost him. He stopped a few yards from Lambeth and sank against a low rock breathing hard, his leg straight out. "I'd say my leg's stiffed up for good, fella. You fixed it for fair, all right."

Lambeth was still staring in a blank daze, and now he said uncertainly, "Ah—Kane."

Brazos hammered his fist against his right thigh. "No feeling, not a goddam tickle. Worse than killing, ganting a man up so the world can poke a finger at him."

Lambeth was blinking and silent, reaching for comprehension, and slowly his face hardened with it. "Go ahead and shoot," he said coldly.

"I'll tell you, Lambeth—" Brazos settled his rifle butt to the ground, fisted his hands around the muzzle and leaned forward. "I'm going to break both your knees and then both elbows, one at a time. No hurry, just wanted you to know."

"Kane, you're a fool. You can't—"

"Why, you damned jughead. Why you think we pulled you way back here? Anybody who hears the shots'll be far enough off not to come running. Gives me all the time in the world, and Pima'll say a couple Montalvos jumped us and did the job on you. Won't be enough left of you to say otherwise."

Lambeth swung a wild stare at Simon Jack; a belated understanding flooded his face, and then a bitter acceptance.

"The Pima's my good compadre. Saved his life a long time back, and he owed me one. Threw Keogh off my trail, then hunted me out himself and tended me and packed in grub."

"And set this up for you," Lambeth said slowly, bitterly. "I see."

Brazos snorted quietly. "Not by a lot, you don't. Who was it said there's one like you born every minute?"

"What does that mean?"

Brazos laughed and shook his head. "Still got you in the dark, have they? You think any ragheel drifter is crazy enough to fool with a rich man's wife? Hell, they set it up gambling you'd be dumb enough to think so. My pay was to be five hundred dollars and a running start—why I left my horse tied at the rail outside the house. Didn't figure you'd take me away from the house. What else I didn't figure was Pinto being on hand to pull down on me when I dropped you. Reckon they had to shut me up for safekeeping."

"They?" One of Lambeth's hands made a fist. "Who is they?

Brazos shook his head in mild despair. "All right, I'll spell it out. Charley Starr and that woman you . . ." He paused chuckling. "I tell you, boy, she should be married to him, all what I seen."

Lambeth drew a shuddering breath and let it out, saying tonelessly, "You're lying."

Brazos eyed him disgustedly. "Well, you're a caution for sure."

"You'll twist the knife any way you can, any way at all."

Brazos shook his head cheerfully. "Forget it. Anyhow you want to take it is fine with me. What concerns me, those two set it up for me as well as you. Now I set it up for you, and their turn comes next. I got all the time in the world, and the Pima to help. About you, now."

"Gently, my friend. You will open your hands and drop the rifle. I would not touch that knife, Simon Jack."

Ramon Velez had moved into sight as he spoke, from behind the first bend; he was afoot. His carbine was beaded on Brazos. *A good piece of timing,* Brazos thought, letting his rifle clatter to the stony ground. Velez half-lowered his rifle. "Senor, take his pistol." Lambeth did not move, his eyes fixed almost stupidly on Brazos. Velez tramped over, lifted Brazos' gun from holster and rammed it into his own belt, then took the Pima's knife. Lambeth roused a little, staring at Velez.

"Ramon, did you hear any of that?"

"Enough." Velez murmured. "I had suspected something like this. Kane and the Pima were ver' friendly, and lately the Pima acts ver' sly; I think maybe he knows where Kane is and helps him. So when I saw him and you go off alone, I followed."

"Not that!" Lambeth checked his harsh speech, scrubbing

127

a hand over his face. "Lucky thing, of course. Thank you for that. I meant what he said about . . . about Mrs. Lambeth."

Velez nodded with careful reserve. "A little, senor."

"Well, what do you think?"

Velez pursed his lips, seeming to consider. He shrugged. "It is empty talk, I think. He wanted to needle you."

Lambeth turned his intent stare back on Brazos, nodding slowly, and Brazos thought, *He wants to believe it, but he's not sure.* Lambeth came to stand above him, closing his fist.

"Kane, you were lying, weren't you?"

"You jughead, why should I lie?"

He saw the blow coming, and made no effort to avoid it. He felt it explode full on his jaw and he tasted blood, and it hurt enough to make him try to roll with the second blow. It caught him solidly on the temple and knocked him sideways off the rock. "That's enough, senor," Velez said sharply.

Lambeth panted, "Yes—waste of time," as he picked up Brazos' rifle, swiftly levering it. Velez' broad bulk moved with amazing speed; he caught the barrel and wrested the weapon away.

"Mayordomo, you are acting the fool," he declared harshly. "Think of that same senora and her grief if you go to prison. Think!"

Lambeth swayed on his feet, his face colorless. "Give him a gun, then."

"No. It will be no different. The man is hurt, and you could not claim self-defense if you push it. These two will go to prison for what they've tried here. But first we should take Kane to your senora; let him say it again and hear her name him a liar."

"No. Damn it, man, why?"

"Because a doubt is a little barb that works deep and makes much poison. It is so with any man, and you are a man."

"I don't . . ." Lambeth paused, his face working strangely. "Suppose you're right. Get rid of it once and for all, eh? Very well. All right, let's get it over."

With Brazos and Simon Jack paired off in the lead, the four of them struck out from Blanco Canyon southeast for Nugget headquarters. *So far, so good,* Brazos thought, counting a split lip a small price for that much. By now Starr and his tough nuts should have quit for the day and returned to the ranch. *At least they'll get there before we do; now if Keogh comes through.*

Shortly they angled onto the wagon road between Nugget and Diablo, and Brazos glanced idly south at the crest of a timbered hill. Keogh and Pepe Garcia should be watching from there. A horse mounted by a bulky double shape was already moving down this way, and he smiled. Velez drew Lambeth's attention to the riders.

"I see them. Pull up." There was a bare patience in Lambeth's voice; only curiosity held him.

In a minute they came onto the road, Pepe mounted behind Keogh's saddle. "I was coming on to your place," Keogh said with a curt nod. "The Mex here came to me with a story, one you'd better listen to. In case," he added ironically, "you hadn't heard."

"What?"

"He'll tell it himself." The sheriff settled a grim eye on Brazos. "Just now I'd like to hear how you got Kane."

Lambeth explained with a nervous impatience what Keogh already knew, and then Pepe began. He said haltingly that of late wolves had troubled his sheep. He had tracked them to the north end of the basin when night had caught him. This was three days ago. He had camped under the rimrock hard by Blanco Canyon when the sound of cattle on the move had wakened him. Out of pure curiosity he had left his camp to work in close till he could make out the six cows. There was enough moonlight to show the men who were driving them. "There were two, the ones called Starr and Sholto, and they drove the cows into the canyon. That is all."

Keogh glanced at Lambeth. "Sounds almighty like Mike O'Brien was right."

"You had better make that plainer." There was a glaze of sweat on Lambeth's face, and he saw it plainly enough.

"Mike thought somebody on the other side had framed things up for him. Only he blamed you, and I don't think so. You're green, Lambeth, and not quite a damned fool till you get a wrong-edged bit in your teeth. I'd say that sums you up, and I could be wrong. I can tell better when I've talked to Starr."

"A bit too convenient, isn't this, coming from a Montalvo man? Damn it, why should he keep still about it till now? He must have heard about his patron getting the blame—Ramon, where were Starr and Sholto three nights ago?"

"Gone to town, mayordomo, to get a drink they said."

"I was scare'," Pepe muttered unhappily. "I was ver' scare of these gringos, who rough me up once. Only this Brazos Kane, the man beside you, saved my life. Later I have felt bad, thinking on all this. Now I talk."

Watching Lambeth's face, recalling Velez' words of how

a little barb could work deep, Brazos thought, *Now he's getting the gaff a sight harder.* And it would sink a sight deeper before this was done, but there was no other way.

Lambeth said dully, "I think we'd better get on to Nugget," and kicked his horse into motion. The rest of them fell in behind him, Keogh and Velez keeping a token guard on Brazos and the Pima.

The sun was deep in the west, the shadows of men and horses elongated to grotesque streaks, as they came into Nugget. The windows of the cookshack glimmered with oily light, and Keogh said idly, "The crew's at supper, eh? Might be handy to fetch Charley Starr along to the house." At Lambeth's sharp glance, he said offhandedly, "Starr'll have to give some answers anyway. From what you said, Kane claims—"

"There's a reasonable explanation for all this—has to be!"

"In that case, you shouldn't object to us hearing 'em both at the same time—Starr's and your wife's."

"There's an explanation," Lambeth muttered. "All right."

They pushed on to the cookshack and dismounted there. A clink of tinware and faint talk drifted from inside. Keogh started toward the door, but it opened as he reached for the latch. Charley Starr bulked in the lamplight, his pale stare shuttling across them. "Now what's all this?" His gaze touched Brazos, and he murmured, "Well, well."

Keogh drew his gun and cocked it in one swift motion. "Back off."

Starr's eyes narrowed; he backed deeper into the bunkroom, Keogh pressing him gently. He said flatly, "Stand up, all of you." He moved his gunbarrel, and there were mutterings and shufflings as Starr's warriors came to their feet. Keogh swiftly disarmed Charley, tossing his gun on the table. He motioned sharply. "The rest of you too, and quick."

There was a thick silence, except for the clatter of weapons, one by one, on the boards.

Lambeth said irritably, "See here, Keogh, you're going a bit too far."

"I don't think so. From all I've heard, I might have to arrest the lot before I leave here, and I don't mean to see 'em unduly tempted."

There was an outbreak of ominous mutters, and Charley Starr said with startled anger, "What the hell do you mean?"

"You'll find out. Get outside." Keogh stepped aside carefully, and Starr hunched his head between his shoulders and wrathfully tramped out. The cook was standing open-mouthed

130

in the kitchen door, and Keogh said, "Get a sack, Coosie, and collect their iron."

Stu Sholto wheeled, awkwardly as a shambling bear, toward the table, and Keogh tilted his gun downward a half-inch and put a shot into it. Sholto froze in position, eying the bullet's splintered track.

"You-all are a nervous man," Keogh said. "You better get outside where I can keep seeing you."

The cook, wearing a pleased grin on his tough face, appeared with a floursack and began dropping the guns into it. Brazos thought with relief, *Well, that's over. He's pulled their teeth.* Forestalling trouble from Starr's hardcases meant disarming them before closing the trap on Starr, and he and Keogh had decided that only a hard decisive crowding of them would turn the trick.

"Coosie, take it you had a bellyful of this crowd."

"Keogh, this crowd is higher than a gassy dog. Got a shotgun in my kitchen if you'll want help."

"Fetch it, and leave their guns in there. Garcia'll watch 'em with you till I get back."

Pepe's ugly face smiled pleasantly as he stepped into the bunkroom, his old muzzle-loader tucked under his arm. Brazos lifted down his crutch, slung by a cloth strap from his saddle horn, and swung into the lead as they headed for the main house. He and Simon Jack, Starr and Sholto were looseherded ahead of Keogh and Velez. Lambeth, impatient with the delay, had already gone on to the house. As Brazos palmed open the door, he heard Lila Mae say plaintively, "But what's to deny? Honey, I just don't see—"

She was pacing agitatedly back and forth by the fireplace, and now she halted as the men filed in. Her eyes dilated faintly and went emerald-hard, then veiled with a half-lidded caution. "Evening there, Mr. Keogh." She gave Brazos a smile of open malice. "See you finally found him."

"Evening. Yes'm, and more than I bargained for." Keogh prodded his four captives over to the wall by the fireplace, and stepped back with his gun ready. He looked almost benignly at Lila Mae. "I wouldn't say you're making too much sense to her, Mr. Lambeth."

"I declare, if that's not so, Mr. Keogh. He came in with a lot of wild talk about something going on he doesn't understand. Well, I surely don't, either."

"To start with, ma'am, this Kane claims you and Starr set it up for Kane to kill your husband." Keogh went on, talking quietly and easily, and Lambeth's pallor deepened with the

131

hammerblows of his soft words. Charley Starr stood with his feet apart and his arms folded, looking faintly bored, his face a casual blank. Brazos thought, *That's smart; he'll keep his mouth shut except to deny it if he's asked; he'll let her handle it.* And Lila Mae, handling it with great aplomb, kneaded her handkerchief in her hands, and made shocked and tearful sounds of objection as Keogh talked.

"I declare," she said in a broken little voice. "I've never been so . . . I just don't know what to say." She turned quickly on her husband. "Johnny, how *could* you? How could you listen to such, such vile filthy nonsense?"

Lambeth's jaw shook, but he set it tightly. "I want the truth, Lila Mae. I want to hear it from you. Did you know Starr before he came here?"

"Oh, how can you even *consider*—"

"Reckon what's galling the horse," Keogh intruded easily, "is that Kane was set to kill Mr. Lambeth when Velez happened up. Only reason Kane would lie to a man he was about to do for, 'ud be for pure meanness, which is likely the case. Sort of points up, though, that Kane *is* capable of murder. And while I put no stock in a killer's word, I got to check back as a matter of duty. Let's see. Starr here has quite a few friends over in Soledad. . . ."

"Oh, well." Lila Mae gave an uncertain laugh; a small tension pinched her lips. "Really, if it's so very important, Mr. Starr and I did have a brief acquaintance a long while ago."

"Lila." Lambeth's eyes were stricken and imploring.

"Now just you wait," she said sharply. "You knew I was a businesswoman before we met. I did spend some time in the West, and I did invest in a business with Mr. Starr in Albuquerque. It . . . it was a gambling establishment to be sure. All perfectly legal, and . . . honey, don't look at me that way. After a time I did realize that Mr. Starr was tied in with an unsavory enterprise or two that a lady shouldn't be remotely connected with, and that was when I sold my share in the business and came to New Orleans. But when this trouble began to flare up here, I just naturally thought of him, so . . ." She looked on the verge of tears. "As things turned out, wasn't I right now?"

"Lila, I'm trying to understand. Why didn't you tell me? And why lie about it?"

"But Johnny, how *could* you understand, all your fine upbringing and proper ways? You couldn't know how a girl trying to make her way all alone in the world has to bend propriety just a bit. And standards are so very different here in the West."

Lambeth was shaking his head passionately. "I don't care about any of that! I can understand, if it's important, why you were afraid to tell me. All I want to know is whether the rest of . . . what Kane claimed, is a lie."

She looked at him with a scornful dignity. "It certainly is. I need hardly add that I've never maintained, at any time, more than a purely business acquaintance with Mr. Starr."

Velez, standing by the doorway, said stolidly, "That is not what my wife says. She has seen—"

This unexpected deflating of her grand moment caught Lila Mae totally off-guard. "That lyin' greaser—!" she burst out with a hating shrillness, and made a tardy recovery by finishing in a soft and helpless way, "—woman. Of course no gentleman would take the word of . . ."

Her voice trailed off, and Brazos saw the appalled shock in John Lambeth's face. One break in her composure had brought the fantasy down in ruin, and now Brazos turned up his last card, playing it on what Delores Velez had seen. He put in idly, "Now that's a real caution, considering what the Pima told me. He says Miz Lambeth offered him a thousand dollars to lay for Charley Starr and put a bullet in him. I wonder why, if her and Starr's so friendly. You sure that's what she said, Pima?"

"Hunh, plenty sure," Simon Jack nodded. "She say, not trust other men do job; they all Starr friend. Wantem dead sure."

Charley Starr unfolded his arms and let them fall stiffly. His mask broke to a swift unthinking passion that made it plain he hadn't one illusion about Lila Mae. "Why you cheating bitch," he said with a murderous calm. "So that's how you were going to cut me out of it."

CHAPTER SEVENTEEN

LILA MAE shot a look of stricken fear at her husband that was probably unfeigned, but she was already dissembling it into a calculating recovery. Lambeth's face said it was too late, and she took a faltering step toward him. "Johnny? Johnny, can't you see what they've gone and done? It's all a pack of lies, honey—"

Her second step took her within arm's length of Starr, and Brazos started to give a belated warning, as going past Starr, she moved between him and Keogh's gun. Starr's hand shot out and closed on her arm. Her scream of surprise and pain was cut off as he swung her back against his chest. His left hand held her with a crushing pressure, and in his right hand, suddenly, the lamplight twinkled blue along a small pocket pistol. In the empty reflex of the moment Brazos thought obscurely that a gambler might wear such a gun sleeve-rigged to drop into his palm at the snap of his wrist.

"Always been your luck, puss, that men were created idiots," Starr said between his teeth, the cruel nudge of his gun against her throat cutting her breath to a strangled sigh. "That should keep you alive awhile, as long as I say. These idiots won't watch a woman get her throat torn open, will you, sheriff? Don't talk; let the gun fall. Velez, lift yours out with your left hand and toss it over here."

Keogh did not move for the space of a long breath, then opened his fist and let the gun thud to the floor. Velez slowly drew his weapon and tossed it underhand; it bounced across the deep rug and stopped a yard from Stu Sholto's feet.

"Pick them up, Stu, and hand me one. Now it's your turn, sheriff—we're going outside and you'll tell Coosie and the Mex to put up their guns."

Brazos had calculated the distance to the lamp burning on its low table to his right, knowing he would never reach it in time. Carefully he slipped his hand up to the armcrotch of his crude staff, and then sidestepping, swept the crutch up, deflecting its butt end into a horizontal arc that met the lamp chimney. It shattered; the heavy lamp crashed to the floor,

134

and the room plunged instantly into the gloom of the increasing twilight.

Brazos let his bad leg give way as he stepped, and he melted to the floor as the blast of Starr's gun came. He was unhit, and twisted onto his side as a flare of oil-fed flame burst across the rug. It showed Simon Jack close to Sholto. Velez must have slipped Simon Jack his knife in an unguarded moment, for it flashed in the Pima's fist—the beefy Stu's cry ended in a choked gurgle as the long blade was sheathed between his ribs.

Sholto's massive form pitched across the blazing rug, the impact trembling the house, and his body partly smothered the flame. As it took again, the dance of confused light showed Charley Starr edging along the wall toward the side window. Abruptly and savagely he flung Lila Mae away from him, and her light weight was spun hard against the fireplace. A soft gasping moan left her, and that was all, as she sank to the floor.

Starr fired once, wildly, and made a wheeling lunge for the half-open window. His hurtling dive carried him across the sill, and his boots struck the sash; then he was through the window and gone.

Keogh on his knees cursed bitterly, groping in the fitful light for the gun Stu had dropped. It had bounded across the floor to stop almost by Brazos' shoulder. He closed his hand around it and climbed to his feet, ignoring his crutch. His leg would bear his weight if he held it stiff, and he started at a dogged hobble for the door. Velez caught at his arm. "Wait, amigo!"

Brazos straight-armed Velez in the chest, knocking him away, and went out the door. He heard Keogh shout, "What the hell, he got the gun?" Brazos moved away at a painful trot, all his attention on Starr who was a good twenty yards ahead of him, lining for the bunkhouse where their horses were still tied. He was limping in his run and must have hurt himself going through the window. *So he has to try for a horse,* Brazos thought tightly, and brought his gun up. But he held fire in the swift and fading twilight and lurched on, setting his teeth against the pain shooting into his thigh.

The bunkhouse door opened suddenly, and against the light Pepe Garcia swung up his long rifle. Its roar cannonaded across the dusk, and Starr hauled up in his tracks. He shot once, but Pepe had already sidestepped out of the doorway. *Not shooting light,* Brazos thought, but he raised his gun to the end of his reach and, gripping his wrist, squeezed the shot gently off.

Starr jerked as a man might at an insect's bite, and pivoting around, shot blindly. Finding himself in a crossfire now, cut off from the horses, he broke at right angles for the rise of ridge behind the house. Brazos set his teeth in his lip and carefully shot again, and thought then, *Save your shots and run him down; he's got a bunged leg too.* Both Keogh and Velez were coming at a run across the yard, Keogh cursing bitterly. Brazos had already settled into a limping trot for the ridge.

Once Starr hit the timber-flanked slope, he might lose himself securely in the dark. A minor sprain would not stop a desperate man from covering many miles by morning, and before then he might pick up a horse at one of the small ranches. He could be across the east pass by dawn, and the man who tried to stop him would face a cornered and dangerous animal. *But he's running scared now; get above him and you can crowd him back to the open.*

Brazos cut for the timber in a straight short line to reach it ahead of Starr who was quartering toward the slope in a wide blind angle. Looking back as he reached the fringe of timber, he was surprised that Velez and the sheriff were not close behind, then realized they would be going after some guns. *Maybe you should wait on them, it's a fool's play.* But a hot determination was in him: Starr was his to take dead or alive.

He plunged into the timber and tackled the steep slope in a lunging stride. His breath whistled through his teeth, and exertion triggered a savage pulse behind his eyes. His leg crawled with fiery pain, and he couldn't tell if the strain had reopened his wound. He drew up in the solid blackness of the arching pines, and braced his hand against one till the spotty haze cleared from his eyes, listening. He had chosen a brush-free line of ascent, and Starr had not. Below and off to his left, Brazos heard a panicked thrashing in the brush as Starr breasted it climbing.

Brazos veered to his left and threaded silently through the trees, working north and slightly downslope to cross Starr's line of advance. He crouched painfully low as he passed into the brush-clogged scrub pine, knowing that Charley would pick him up at once. Starr shot once into the trees; Brazos fired back, hoping the knowledge that he was blocked would deflect Charley's flight off the ridge and its timber. He paused, sounding out Starr's renewed direction from the crackling brush, and then followed. The man was heading in a line that would carry him northeast of Nugget headquarters to free and open ground, and now it was a matter of who could move faster.

As the timber thinned away toward the ridgebase, Brazos saw Starr's dim shape a good forty yards ahead on the open flat. Charley was limping hard and he was bent half-double, clutching his hit shoulder. *He won't make it far, but if he has the sense to lay up before he drops, it'll be a sight harder taking him.* Brazos remembered now that a vast shallow bowl filled by a fifty-yard radius of rock and brush lay just ahead. Charley was heading for there, he guessed, in hopes of temporarily losing himself, later to slip out unseen while darkness held.

A deep shadow where the flat dipped sharply away marked the rim of the bowl, and in a moment he saw Starr drop over it and disappear. Brazos pulled up short to take his breath and weigh his next move. He caught a drift of shouts from the ridge. Keogh and Velez had seen him head there, and would confine their search there unless a shot or a hallo pulled them back. He could hail them and keep Starr pinned within the bowl, or he could go down after him. Unhesitatingly he moved forward, but skirting wide of the point he had seen Starr vanish. A sheen of early moonlight was on the terrain now, enough to skyline him for the moment he'd need to go over the rim. If Starr had laid up to rest below, he'd be watching and ready.

Brazos came up on the north side of the declivity, then hobbled for its edge and let his feet drop abruptly into the blackness. He dug in the heel of his sound leg, flailing at the gravel that rattled down before him. He hit the bottom and went belly-down in soft sand, tensed for a shot. It did not come, and he inched onto his rump, thinking, *Now he's getting careful. And now we'll see what sort of nerves he's got.*

Patiently he let his eyes adjust to the darkness, the thin moonlight outlining monolithic boulders and clumped stalks of dead brush. *Now,* he thought, and after slipping off his boots, eased stealthily into the boulder field in his sock feet, carefully avoiding the dry thickets. *Got to pull his fire.* He stooped and felt for a pebble, and straightening, lobbed it high to his right. He waited, feeling sweat break on his belly, and when no betraying shot answered him, thought, *You too, eh, Charley? Question of who spooks first. Maybe this will do it.*

He dug into his pocket for his clasp knife, opened both blades, and overhanded it away, this time to his left. It struck rock with a startling, metallic clang, followed by a sharp

137

splintering of brush. This subsided at once, and he grinned. *Near enough to give him a start, and puts him about five yards to your right.* He remained motionless, straining his ears into the onrunning silence.

"God damn you to hell, Kane!"

Charley's voice came clear and sudden, and Brazos forced his quivering muscles still. *Not yet.* He raised himself a cautious few inches and studied the rocks through the screening brush, and located a black pocket between two slablike boulders. *That's it.*

"Speak out, you yellow bastard!"

Don't waste your wind, Charley.

"Listen—Kane. I have money, five figures banked away, and it's all yours. We ride out of here together; all you have to do is fetch two horses."

You can't take him from the front or the sides, but that pocket looks open to the rear.

"What do you say, Kane?"

Bent low, Brazos slipped away across the bare rocks, unable to tell whether an unknown angle of his circle might expose him to Starr's gun. *This close, it's no time for cold feet; just don't think about it.* He made a stiff-legged and awkward run across a last open break. He came noiselessly against the outer side of one of the massive slabs that sheltered Starr, and there was not ten feet between them.

"Kane?"

Starr's voice was startling in its nearness, and he hugged the slab hardly breathing. After a quarter-minute Starr said with a flat taunting edge, "About that money, it really is yours. Want to hear about that?"

Anything to force my hand; he needs a target. Yet the words held Brazos baffled and unmoving, a cold tingle fingering his spine.

"The old man, Kane. Melaven. Your partner. I'm the man you want, you chuckleheaded fool."

Brazos pressed his sweating face to the rough stone, holding in. *He's not lying, or he wouldn't know.* And two secondary details jogged him with significance: Starr's schooled blandness and the dexterous way he'd palmed the gambler's pistol. His man's pallid thinness and foreign accent made sharp discrepancies, but weeks of hard ranch work could give a man appetite and color, while the bartender Seeley, not a bright soul, could have mistaken a lisp for an accent.

"You're doubtful? Only your guilty party'll know where

138

the money is—safe in the bank at Boulder, way over by the border. That's the truth, Kane, now come ahead."

Brazos came swiftly around the bulge of rock, and he saw Charley's broad back.

"Kane. Shoot, God damn you!"

"Right behind you, Charley, but don't make me."

He did not expect resistance from Starr, who was caught on his haunches cramped between the rocks, his back turned. But Charley made his try, swiveling on his heels and coming upright while his gun was still arcing around. Brazos shot him in the shoulder.

The blow drove Starr against the rock, where he hung slumped. His chin dropped to his chest and a vast sighing breath left him. "Oh, God," he said tiredly. "I wish . . ." A strong effort jerked him erect, and his gun came up. An old cynicism had kept Brazos' gun unlowered, and its butt bucked against his palm.

Starr folded backward till the rock caught his hips, hugging his arms across his chest while his face tilted slowly to the moon, a crooked smile fluting his lips. He went down sitting, still holding himself, and rolled on his side with his knees pulled up. Brazos sat abruptly on the sand, and a limp weariness washed through him. He heard the wet gurgle of Charley's last breathing which, after a minute or so, ended.

He was aware that Keogh, drawn by the shots, was calling his name, and did not answer at once. He ran back over it in his mind, thinking, *I gave him his chance,* and was satisfied. *Not the way it started out, Pop, but you wouldn't give a damn. And you never did.* And he thought: *That's the difference between us. So long, Pop.*

CHAPTER EIGHTEEN

AN HOUR LATER Starr's hardcases moved out in a body, Liam Keogh and six Montalvo vaqueros riding a close rear guard on them. Keogh had laid down a hard ultimatum to the lot, and with their leadership broken, none were disposed to argue. They were to be out of the Two Troughs country by dawn. Keogh would see them as far as the south pass where their guns, bulging the floursack slung from his pommel, would be returned. He touched his hat in parting salute, riding past the lighted doorway of the bunkhouse. Brazos stood there with Mike and Raquel O'Brien, Ramon Velez and Simon Jack, and they watched the riders till they were gone.

O'Brien had waited a bare hour before giving his vaqueros an order, and they had come to Nugget in a solid bunch. Raquel had followed them at a distance. It was over by then, and no harm done; and Keogh needed help to herd off Starr's warriors.

A chill wind dipped across the buildings, bearing its token of unmelted snow in the high Diablos. Brazos felt the girl shiver against his arm. "We'll step inside."

They entered the bunkroom and Velez shut the door, then went to the potbelly stove and stirred up the dying coals, adding a few cedar lengths. He said over his shoulder, "I think it will not be hard to get back the old crew, now. All of them are hunting jobs around the basin, and tomorrow I will look them up."

A silence, except for the crackling stove, followed his words. Brazos sat at the table and laid his hat on it, and passed a hand over the red bristle of his unshaven jaw. He felt bone-tired, though it was mostly reaction. There was something he felt bound to do. His thought touched without pleasure on the tarp-covered bodies of Starr and Stu Sholto in the tack barn, but that was not it. He lifted his eyes, aware of Raquel's and Mike's quiet regard, and he said: "A dirty night's work."

"No," Mike said. "A good one's." He slacked onto the bench opposite Brazos, folding his scarred hands on the table. "The life of a coyote or two is small potatoes next what you saved the lot of us from."

"I meant Lambeth."

Raquel had come to his side, and her hand lay gently on his shoulder. "There was no other way."

"I set it up that way, all to tear a man apart. You can do a thing too damned well."

"Time'll help that; it'll help us all," said Mike O'Brien. "Come on, lad, we'll be getting along home."

Brazos shook his head, coming to his feet. "Something I have to do first."

"Ah," Mike said softly, "I'd let the man alone. What can you tell him that he'll want to hear?"

"Nothing. It has to be said, that's all."

Leaving them, he headed through the windy darkness for the main house, where a dim light burned in the parlor window. Hesitating on the veranda, he thought, *get it over*, and went in. Lambeth had his armchair pulled up by the settee, and appeared to be dozing with his head on his chest. Brazos looked, not wanting to, at the blanket-covered form on the settee. One woman and her greed had brought near-disaster to a peaceful country, and maybe she had got only her deserving. The trouble with retribution was that it could touch the wrong people. Lila Mae alive, exposed for what she was, might have wiped herself from the mind of a man she'd betrayed from the start. Lila Mae dead, leaving a thousand warm false memories with him, was a grieved martyr to her ambitions.

"Lambeth."

John Lambeth jerked slightly, and lifted his head. "Hullo. Kane?"

Brazos moved across the deep carpet till he stood by the divan, only then looking directly at Lambeth. "Sorry. That's no good, but I'm sorry."

"Sorry?" Lambeth blinked, as if to wrench his attention to the word. "Ah. The best laid plans, eh, the hitch you never look for. How could you know that my wife would strike her head on the mantel, and—oh, Starr's doing of course. Still your little scheme led up to it, didn't it?"

"Yes."

Lambeth passed a hand over his eyes, tiredly. "I suppose you think I'm an utter ass."

Brazos shifted his feet, scowling at his hat in his hands. "Man has a right to one thing in his life that doesn't bear much reason. A lot of men have given up their lives for a hellsmear of wrongheaded notions."

141

"Don't know." Lambeth rubbed his eyelids slowly. "All a damned muddle now. But I think I knew; perhaps did from the start. The little things, you know. Hard not to tell rather a good deal of a person you live with intimately. A man sees what he wants to see, but even if I hadn't . . ." He let his hand drop. "So, she even approached the Pima to have her true partner put out of the way."

Brazos shook his head. "No. It might have come to that, was all. We knew her and Starr were on the outs over something, and it was a handy way to break Starr down." Brazos paused, hating to say it, but he did. "He was bound to believe it, knowing her."

Lambeth exhaled gently. "Yes. And the rest?"

All true, Brazos told him, except that he had been duped, not hired, into the duel that was to have taken Lambeth's life; and Pepe Garcia had been nowhere about when Starr and Sholto had hazed the Nugget steers into Blanco Canyon for that night's work. A lot of what had happened, he added, could have been Starr's idea.

"Don't grease the axle, Kane." Lambeth formed a painful smile. "Not necessary, even if I'd known. I loved her, you see. Afraid I still do. If she'd shown her true colors, had handed me a gun and told me flatly to do the job on myself, it wouldn't really change anything. Odd thing about that, I might have done it." He stared at the blanketed form. "All I want now is never to see this place again. I'll be getting away as soon as possible, and never mind whether I can find a buyer. That loss I can easily afford."

Something that Starr had said nudged at Brazos' tired mind then. Twelve thousand dollars that was his lay intact in the bank at Boulder, and with the law's help he could reclaim it. To bring up that blood money under the circumstances was not pleasant, but he was nothing if not realistic. Pride and poverty made a sorry mixture, and he wasn't about to take the charity help he knew Mike would offer the man his daughter had chosen.

"No need for that," he answered Lambeth. "I have some money banked away, and I want the place. Twelve thousand won't take it by far, but I can arrange a long-term—"

Lambeth cut him off impatiently. "I'm independently wealthy, Kane, and I told you how it is. Twelve thousand will take it—headquarters, land and cattle. I'll be out of here within two days, so sound me out before then."

His eyes retreated into memory, and Brazos left him that way. Outside, he paused to breathe in the cold wind deeply.

Strange how a man came to take being alive for granted—eating and sleeping and working. And trouble. But facing it alone was the hard part, and he had always taken this for granted too. *No more of that.*

She was standing outside the bunkhouse as he neared it. The voices of O'Brien and Velez droned faintly from inside, and she closed the door on them now. Light from a window kindled warmly on her face, her eyes and lips. "Was it very hard?"

"Not so hard. That'll wait."

He took her by the arms, their round softness bringing an instant warmth to his hands. Her face came up and a quick pulse stirred in her throat. "Now we'll go home?"

"We're home. That'll keep too. Now . . ."

69-8-2

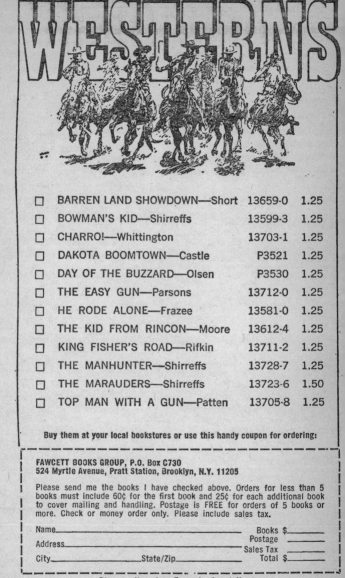

WESTERNS

☐	BARREN LAND SHOWDOWN—Short	13659-0	1.25
☐	BOWMAN'S KID—Shirreffs	13599-3	1.25
☐	CHARRO!—Whittington	13703-1	1.25
☐	DAKOTA BOOMTOWN—Castle	P3521	1.25
☐	DAY OF THE BUZZARD—Olsen	P3530	1.25
☐	THE EASY GUN—Parsons	13712-0	1.25
☐	HE RODE ALONE—Frazee	13581-0	1.25
☐	THE KID FROM RINCON—Moore	13612-4	1.25
☐	KING FISHER'S ROAD—Rifkin	13711-2	1.25
☐	THE MANHUNTER—Shirreffs	13728-7	1.25
☐	THE MARAUDERS—Shirreffs	13723-6	1.50
☐	TOP MAN WITH A GUN—Patten	13705-8	1.25

Buy them at your local bookstores or use this handy coupon for ordering: